WITH VACANT POSSESSION?

By Gillian Baxter

With Vacant Possession? Copyright © 2017 by Gillian Baxter. All Rights Reserved.

All rights reserved. No part of this book may be reproduced in any form or by any electronic or mechanical means including information storage and retrieval systems, without permission in writing from the author. The only exception is by a reviewer, who may quote short excerpts in a review.

Cover images: istock: Abramova Kseniya
Alphotographic

This book is a work of fiction. Names, characters, places, and incidents either are products of the author's imagination or are used fictitiously. Any resemblance to actual persons, living or dead, events, or locales is entirely coincidental.

Gillian Baxter

Printed in the United Kingdom

First Printing: March 2018

CONTENTS

Chapter One 2
Chapter Two 16
Chapter Three 33
Chapter Four 45
Chapter Five 60
Chapter Six 73
Chapter Seven 87
Chapter Eight 99
Epilogue...four years later 120

CHAPTER ONE

The road seemed to have been climbing for miles. Ahead the rising surface glistened in the headlights, damp from the last shower, and on either side banks rose into the featureless darkness of the open moorland. The old Transit was labouring, its engine roaring, and there was a smell of hot metal. At the wheel, her arms aching from the long drive and her back sore from the upright old seat, Patsy peered into the darkness, hoping for somewhere to pull off the road to rest both her and the lorry. There it was...a capital P on a blue background... Parking, and the crest of the hill was ahead. Thankful, Patsy hauled the wheel round and the Transit lurched onto rough ground. A wire sheep fence showed in the headlights, and a stretch of flattish hard standing with a litter bin in a corner. Patsy braked, pulled on the handbrake, and switched off the engine. The silence was miraculous, flooding into the cab and singing in Patsy's ears. The lorry swayed as, behind, the two horses shifted in their stalls, and one of them, David, for Patsy knew both their voices intimately, whinnied. Surprisingly there was an answering whinny from outside, and Patsy saw movements in the dimness ahead. She switched on the headlights again and saw a group of moor ponies, their eyes shining in the light, staring towards her from a track which led away from the car park onto the open mountain country beyond.

The sudden flood of light had startled the ponies. They threw up their heads and shied, turning away, their small, stocky bodies shining grey, brown, and dappled as they moved. There were sheep out there as well, startled like the ponies, white shapes settled for sleep in dips in the ground and under rocks. Patsy switched her lights off again and opened the cab door. The sweet, cold upland air flowed in, scented with earth and growing things, and a tinge of sheep. Patsy slid stiffly off her seat and lowered herself carefully to the ground, feeling her muscles crack and give after many hours behind the wheel. Eight hours, with only a short stop at the motorway services beyond the Severn Bridge. She deserved a few moments to stretch before the last tortuous bit through the lanes to the farm...her farm.

Flinging back her head, Patsy stared up at the vast sky. Mackerel clouds were drifting across a three-quarter moon, throwing strange shadows. It felt like the top of the world up here. Far below, a cluster of lights showed a distant town, and a blinking red light high in the air was the top of a communications mast. Was she mad...coming here alone like this, to start a new life at sixty? Katy had thought so. She had told her mother that many times since Patsy had first told her about her plan to buy Bryn Uchaf.

'But it's what I want,' Patsy reminded herself. 'Katy has her life...she's made that clear often enough. Now I'm going to have mine, even if sixty is a bit late to start doing my own thing.'

It was time to get back into the cab, out of this great, intimidating wilderness of night and moorland and moonlight, and drive on down to the cosy farmhouse that she had fallen in love with after seeing it advertised in the *Telegraph* at a ridiculously low price, even for West Wales.

The journey took another half an hour, down from the mountain, then the turning off the B road into the lanes, winding up and down between high banks until she saw the bridge over the stream, and changed down for the lorry to grind up the last short hill to the turning into her own drive, past the faded wooden sign which read 'Bryn Uchaf'.

The Transit turned slowly in, lurching over the pot holes, and crept along between more banks topped by hedges, shaggy even now in March. A white barn owl rose silently from an overhanging branch and drifted away into the darkness, and Patsy saw the cattle grid and gate beside it which led into the yard. The Transit was lurching over the rattling bars of the cattle grid when Patsy saw the figure in front of her, close to the bonnet, only a dark shape in the darker spot between the headlights. She stamped on the brakes so suddenly that, even at their slow speed, the horsebox lurched and bounced to a stop, the engine stalling, and behind her Patsy heard the two horses banging and slipping as they struggled to keep their balance. Shaking, she wound down the window and put her head out.

'Who is it?' she called. 'Are you all right? I almost ran you down.'

There was no reply. Suddenly frightened, Patsy grabbed a torch from the dashboard and scrambled down from the cab. Surely she hadn't really knocked him over?

The torch, dim against the headlights, still showed the dark gap between. There was no-one there. Her legs weak, Patsy bent down to shine the torch under the lorry, but to her utter relief the beam showed nothing but mud. It must have been her imagination, and yet it had been so real...

'Shadows,' Patsy told herself. 'Shadows and tiredness...'

Inside the lorry the horses were pawing anxiously at the floor, and Goliath whinnied.

'All right...hang on a minute...' Patsy climbed back inside, re-started the engine, and drove forward to park alongside the house, with the sloping yard on her right. She was there.

Outside the lorry the silence at first seemed absolute, the silence and the darkness, wrapping her round.

Reaching back into the cab Patsy found her torch again and switched it on. The shadows swung and quivered, and she became aware of the sound of running water, the stream that ran just below the yard. Getting her bearings, Patsy found the outside light switch and the yard lights came on, dim, but enough to make everything seem much more accessible. There was still no sign of anyone about...the yard was deserted.

There were two stables ready in the long stone building that had once been a cowshed, bedded down when Patsy had come down two days earlier with the furniture van. She reached up to undo the bolts which held the horsebox ramp, and lowered it with a crash onto the damp concrete.

David and Goliath were delighted to see the outside world again. David, the elderly brown pony with the creamy coloured nose, was first out, stepping stiffly down the ramp and pricking his ears at the strange smells and shadows. Patsy led him into the nearer of the two stables, while inside the lorry Goliath kicked and pawed and roared that he was being deserted. He would not wait while she untied him, pushing her with his powerful brown and white shoulder, and the moment he felt the rope come free he was off, charging down the box ramp and calling for his friend, who was too busy exploring his new home to reply. Patsy was left staggering on the slippery ramp, the rope jerked out of her hand. By the time she reached the ground Goliath had vanished, although the thump of his hooves and more roars of anguish because he was lost came from the direction of the field. Patsy grabbed a bucket and some pony nuts from the lorry and set off in pursuit.

There was no sign of Goliath in the field. Patsy shouted, and David whinnied in the stable, but the brown and white horse had vanished into the wide darkness. The field was surrounded by banks, mostly topped by hedges, but hurrying along one of them Patsy saw a gap, and scrambled hoof marks going through it. She also heard the not too far distant baaing of disturbed sheep, and a dog began to bark.

'Golly', shouted Patsy. 'Goliath...come on.'

She scrambled through the gap, and saw sheep clustered in a corner, and beyond them the lights of another farm.

'Golly,' called Patsy again, and this time there was a reply.

'I've got him.' The voice was female and Welsh. 'Over by the yard...come to the lights.'

Patsy did as she was told, and found herself at the gate into a wide, floodlit farmyard. A short, stocky woman with curly dark hair was holding Goliath's rope and letting him circle round her, while two black and white collies slipped round after him, low to the ground, like animated shadows themselves.

'Thank you.' Patsy took charge of Goliath. 'I thought I was going to be searching all night. He can be rather a fool.'

'No problem,' the woman assured her. 'I heard him in my sheep, and the dogs cornered him by the gate. You must be the new lady at Emrys's...all the way from London, isn't it?'

'Well, not quite...Surrey...not far from London, though.' Patsy told her. 'I'm Patsy...Patsy Heath.'

'I'm Rhiannon Evans,' Goliath's captor told her. 'You're all on your own, is it? That's brave...I wouldn't like to live all alone. You'll want to get this boy home...wait and I'll come with you...hold the torch. I'll get my wellies.'

With Rhiannon leading the way, Patsy led the anxiously pulling Goliath back across her own field, and into his new stable at last. With David next door, and a nice, soft shavings bed to stand on, Goliath subsided, seeming to deflate, and lay down to roll luxuriously. Patsy gave them both an armful of hay, and turned to the watching Rhiannon, suddenly conscious of how tired she was. Rhiannon seemed to sense it, for she said, 'Better let me come in and make you a cup of tea. You could do with a sit down after that drive, couldn't you now?'

'It...it would be nice.' For some reason, looking at the dark house, Patsy felt that she would be rather glad of company on first going into it. She found the key in her handbag, and led the way round to the front door. The key was large and made of iron, no neat little Yale key, and Rhiannon shone the torch while she pushed it into the lock. The key refused to turn. Patsy twisted and pushed, and began to feel flustered. If she couldn't even get into her new home...

'Let me try.' Rhiannon gently took the key from her. 'Bit stiff, I expect. Come on now, let us in...'

She turned the key, and the lock clicked. The door swung open, and Rhiannon stepped in first and reached for the light switch.

'Know my way around, see,' she said. 'These houses are all alike, and John and me, we visited with Emrys now and again.'

Feeling rather foolish, Patsy followed her along the hall, past the foot of the stairs, and into the back room, which was straight ahead. Another light went on, and Patsy saw her familiar furniture looking awkward in the strange room. There was a green Rayburn cooker on the right in its alcove, the slope of the wooden stairs going up above on the left. The kitchen was on the left as well, through another door, big and rather old-fashioned with its wooden units and deep windowsills, perfect for plants one day, Patsy had thought when she first saw the house. Tonight it struck cold, and Patsy shivered. There was something alien about the atmosphere, waiting and unwelcoming. It was the cold, of course, and the darkness...Patsy saw her electric kettle ready by its switch, and Rhiannon smiled at her.

'You make the tea,' she said, 'While I see can I get that old stove started.'

Patsy was glad to agree. She filled the electric kettle and switched it on, and rooted cups, tea, sugar, and long-life milk out of the box she had left ready. There was kindling and a hod of coal already in the deep, brick alcove beside the Rayburn, and Rhiannon built a fire and set light to it, adjusting the dampers and drawers with the skill of much practice.

'There,' she said. 'Bank it up well when you go to bed, and almost close these two controls, and it should be glowing well in the morning.'

Already there was a faint warmth creeping into the room, and Patsy made the tea and they sat down at the gate-legged table.

'Well now,' said Rhiannon. 'That's better. Will your family be visiting you?'

It was a gentle probe, and Patsy knew that she owed Rhiannon her background.

'My daughter will,' she said. 'She's all the family I have, except a few distant cousins and so on. My husband died, eight months ago.'

'That's hard.' Rhiannon looked sympathetic. 'I'd be lost without my John. I've a son, Gareth, but he's not into farming, a computer man is Gareth, works in Carmarthen. How will you manage, then, all on your own here?'

'I'll get used to it, I'm sure,' Patsy told her. 'My husband...well...he hadn't been well for a long time, so I'm pretty used to managing.'

'Well, any problems, and we're not so far away,' Rhiannon told her. 'I'll write the number down now, before I go, and don't be shy to call us if you need help. It's land line only I'm afraid, the masts don't work well round here. This is a big old place to be all by yourself in, don't go getting scared and feel all alone.'

'Thank you very much.' Patsy was touched by the obvious concern of her new friend. 'It will be different, but somewhere like this is what I've always wanted.'

They finished their tea in a companionable silence. Patsy was starting to feel very tired after the move, and the long drive, and Rhiannon too looked tired. The tea finished, Patsy saw her to the door. On the step Rhiannon hesitated, looking back down the hall.

'A lady from England, now,' she said. 'A long way, and all alone. Brave, is that. You'll not be unwelcome, I'm sure, that wouldn't be right.'

'I I hope I won't.' Patsy was startled. Rhiannon did not seem to be looking at her, but past her, rather, towards the back room with its dark wood and warm alcove, the heart of the house, Patsy had already sensed. Then Rhiannon looked back at her and smiled.

'Don't mind me,' she said. 'I'm sure things will go well for you. Goodnight now, and remember, we're always at home.'

She stepped out of the door and a dark shape slid out of the shadows to meet her. Patsy saw that one of the sheep dogs had followed its mistress across the fields.

'That's Bryn,' Rhiannon told her. 'Looks after me, he does. You should get a dog, be less lonely, and he could help you round up that old horse of yours.'

'Maybe I will,' Patsy told her. It was worth thinking about. She could have all kinds of animals now, with no-one to say they were a liability, as her husband Richard would have done. She waved as Rhiannon went back towards the fields, her torch lighting the way, and Bryn circling round her as if she was a lost sheep he had come to collect. Patsy turned back into the house, closed the back door, and leaned on it, surveying her new domain.

Bryn Uchaf had been described in the advertisement as a holding of sixteen acres, ideal for small-holding or equestrian use. There was a small area of woodland, sloping to a stream, stables, a barn, and outbuildings with plenty of potential, although the advertisement had not specified what this might be. Patsy just intended to live here, with plenty of room for horses, space to breathe, and the pleasure of beautiful surroundings, for Bryn Uchaf was situated in the Pembrokeshire Coast National Park, in the Preseli Hills area. The house was a square, stone farmhouse with four symmetrical rooms upstairs and down, much old wood and rather shabby porches back and front. Now, as Patsy stood there in the silence, the house seemed to be waiting, holding itself apart until it discovered what its new owner was going to make of it. The previous owner's curtains, plain blue cotton, were still at the windows, his plain dark blue carpets on the floors, his worn dark red linoleum in the kitchen. In its alcove the Rayburn was murmuring faintly, but giving out, it seemed to Patsy, less warmth. She checked that the controls were as Rhiannon had advised, and shivered.

'I'm tired,' she said aloud. 'I'll fill a hot water bottle, and get to bed.'

She had done so, and was actually starting to climb the stairs, when the telephone rang, sudden and shrill, shattering the stillness of the house and making Patsy jump. It was still on the floor beside the heavy oak front door, waiting for Patsy to sort her furniture out enough to find it a proper stand. Feeling her back stiffening after the drive, Patsy bent to lift the receiver.

'Mum,' her daughter Katy's voice sounded impatient, 'So you have got there. I've rung and rung, I was starting to think something awful had happened. Are you all right?'

'Yes, fine,' Patsy felt herself being defensive. Katy had never approved of this move. 'Golly dashed off, and a neighbour caught him. She's very nice. We had a cup of tea together, and she said if I needed help she and her husband are very near. So you see, you needn't worry.'

'How can I help worrying when you've gone dashing off like this?' Katy demanded. 'Even Andrew thinks it's something to worry about.'

'I'm glad he cares.' Patsy knew she sounded bitter, but Katy's lightly married boyfriend had long been a sore point. 'Anyway, we've been through all this before, and I'm here now, and I'm going to bed. I'll 'phone you tomorrow and let you know how I'm settling in.'

After putting down the 'phone she could feel the deep weariness enveloping her. A quick wash in the unfamiliar bathroom, and then the one really familiar thing in the house, her own bed, the bed in which she had slept for all of her married life, in which Katy, in a hurry as always, had been born, and in which Richard had suffered the heart attack which had killed him. Warm, soft, full of memories of joy and sorrow, of love and fear, it was the place she could crawl to recover. She was deeply settled, the strange surroundings fading into the background, sinking luxuriously down into the first delicious sleep, when something jerked her awake. The door to her bedroom had swung open, making a slight creak.

'I can't have latched it,' Patsy's mind registered. 'Never mind...it isn't cold...'

She turned over, but suddenly she found herself wide awake again. There was someone in the room. No sound, but a sense of movement, a stirring in the air. Abruptly Patsy sat up, switching on her bedside lamp so hurriedly that she almost knocked it over. There was no-one there. The door was half open, and a draught was moving the previous owner's thin cotton curtains.

'You're imagining things,' Patsy told herself firmly. 'Fine start that is. Now go to sleep.'

Determinedly she switched off the lamp and lay down, pulling the duvet well up to her ears. Outside, comfortingly, Goliath whinnied, calling into the strange night, and David replied with his deep pony whicker. There was an owl giving short, sharp cries somewhere close by, and a murmur of wind rattled a door. Reassured, Patsy slept.

Patsy was woken early the next morning by a series of mournful wails from below her bedroom window which it took her a few minutes to recognise as made by a cat. Stumbling out of bed, she pulled back the thin curtain and peered out. The cold greyness of an early March morning filtered into the room and Patsy found that the jutting back porch cut out any view of what was directly below. Pulling on her dressing gown, she went downstairs to investigate.

The cat was waiting outside the back door, a bedraggled looking little tabby with large, pleading golden eyes in a pinched little face. She had the prominent backbone and big tummy of malnutrition, and Patsy knew that she could not say 'No.'

'But it won't be cat food,' she warned the cat, who had backed away out of reach but was still wailing. 'I'll see what I can find.'

She left the back door open but the cat did not venture further than the step, from where it continued to cry. Searching in one of the boxes, still packed, of tins and packets, Patsy found a tin of sardines and another of stewed steak. Sardines she knew would probably be most popular, but they were rich and might not settle well in a cat as scrawny and desperate as this one seemed to be. Stewed steak, with some bread crumbled in it, seemed a better idea.

The cat certainly didn't complain. She...for Patsy saw that it was a female, crouched down by the saucer, opened her mouth and the food went down as though drawn in by a vacuum cleaner. In approximately two minutes the saucer was clean and the cat was backing away, still gazing at Patsy.

'No more for now,' Patsy told it. 'You'd just be sick. If you want to come back later I'll see what's going.'

The cat seemed to understand her tone of voice, and as Patsy stepped into her wellingtons to go to the horses she turned and slipped away under the bushes which surrounded the small garden.

In the yard Goliath was shouting that he was being starved, hammering his door with one front foot, and Patsy knew that he had heard her voice. Food always came first in Goliath's mind.

The horses fed, Patsy returned to the house to find her own breakfast, and as she closed the back door it struck her that the house felt surprisingly chilly. With a nasty suspicion stirring in her mind Patsy looked at the stove. It sat there, solid and work-worn on its brick hearth, the green enamel of the front streaked here and there with brown, and the once silver covers over the hot plates dark and chipped. The temperature dial on the oven stood at zero. Patsy had the ridiculous feeling that it was testing her. Opening the metal door to the fire box she saw only cold blackness.

'Oh, drat it.' Patsy slammed the metal door and looked at the dampers. Both were pushed hard in...surely Rhiannon had left them open enough to keep a slight draught going? Thankful that she had 'the electric' Patsy switched on her electric kettle and put bread in the toaster. She would deal with the Rayburn later.

It was a busy morning. First Patsy had to explore her fields, and decide which was the most secure for turning out into, then the old bath which served as a water trough had to be cleaned out and the hose with which to fill it had to be dug out from the pile of outdoor equipment in the barn. Turning from the tap Patsy was suddenly riveted by the view from the back of her new home. Beyond the fields the moor began, brown and purple today in the watery March sunlight. Open stretches of lowland swept on and up into the great rise of the bare hills. The high slopes were streaked with silver where water ran down from the tops, and lower patches of blue and silver showed standing water and streams patching the lowland.

'That's what I came for,' said Patsy to herself. 'That, and peace and a different pace of life. Later today...or tomorrow...I'll saddle Goliath and go out to explore.'

At last the field was ready for the horses to go out, and Patsy led them through the gate together. Let loose, Goliath gave David a nudge, urging him to lead the way, and they set off at a trot to explore, Goliath keeping behind David so that any hidden bogeys would get his small, sturdy friend first. Patsy smiled, watching them for a few minutes, and then turned back to face the task of creating some kind of order in the house.

The first task was to re-light the Rayburn. It took ages to rake out all the dead coal, build up a fire with screwed up newspaper and kindling, and then wait, feeding it carefully with coal, until the blaze got hold.

Then Patsy carefully set the dampers as Rhiannon had showed her, and turned to her unpacking.

Gradually the house began to look more like a home. Patsy concentrated on the living room and her bedroom, and by mid-afternoon the major part was done. There was china on the old oak dresser which she had owned for many years, and which went very well with the dark, varnished panelling which shielded the back door, and enclosed the stairs above her head. Books filled the shelves in an alcove, and there was a rug over the carpet inside the door. There were still two boxes of books on the landing, left there by the removal men, and too heavy for her to shift alone, She would sort those out later. She was about to make a cup of tea when she again noticed the chill in the room, and saw that the dial on the Rayburn oven was once more at zero heat. Opening it, Patsy saw the dead coals inside.

'I don't believe it.' Patsy stared at the cold stove. She was sure she had been so careful, and yet both the dampers she thought were properly adjusted were pushed right home, stopping any draught from drawing the fire. She was staring at it, cross with herself, but puzzled, when there was a knock at the front door.

Opening it, Patsy found herself confronting a tall, thin young man with a shock of dark hair dressed in a tee shirt, an old bomber jacket, and torn jeans. For a moment, remembering the threats of life in the south-east, she was tempted to close the door hastily, but then he smiled at her and stepped back a little and Patsy realised that he had guessed what she was thinking.

'I'm Gareth Evans,' he said. 'Mam sent me down to ask if you were managing. I'm home a bit early today.'

So this was the computer buff who worked in Carmarthen. He wasn't in the least what Patsy would have expected, but she could see the likeness now in the smiling dark eyes and the tilt of the head.

'It's very good of you,' she said. 'Actually I am having a bit of a problem. The stove keeps going out.'

'Let's have a look.' Gareth followed her into the living room and across to the stove. 'Look, you've got these dampers closed...it won't draw without a draught.'

'I know,' Patsy told him. 'Your mother explained it all...and I thought I'd got it right...I did re-light it once, and it was going well...'

Gareth was crouching in front of the stove, opening the door, but now he glanced round at her, and Patsy thought that he looked amused.

'Was it now?' he said. 'Well, I'll get it going again for you...and don't let it bother you...it'll settle...get used to you, see?'

As Patsy stared at him he turned back to the open stove. It did not take him as long to get it going again as it had Patsy, and he stood back and smiled at her.

'There you are,' he said. 'I've set the dampers, no reason now for it to go out. Don't stand any nonsense, that's what my Mam would say. Now, is there anything else I can help you with?'

Patsy remembered the boxes of books, and after that Gareth asked if there were any jobs outside, and she thought of the bales of hay inside the horse box which she had been putting off hauling out. It was soon done. In spite of his defection to computers Gareth handled the heavy bales with the easy familiarity of a boy from a farming background. The March afternoon was chilly now, a sharp little wind gusting down from the bare hills, and David and Goliath were at the gate, watching hopefully for Patsy to come and bring them in for tea.

'All right boys, I'm coming,' Patsy opened the gate, and Gareth watched, amused, as she led Goliath in with David trotting past them and on into his own stable.

'It hasn't taken him long to learn where he sleeps,' he said.

'David's clever,' Patsy told him. 'Much cleverer than Goliath. Golly relies on him for security. They were both my daughter Katy's horses before she lost interest.'

Gareth stayed to watch as she fed the horses, and helped her carry hay to them from the bales in the barn.

'Dad will let you have some hay,' he told her. 'You'll be needing some pretty soon.'

'That would be great.' Patsy was relieved. Knowing where to get hay would be one more problem solved. As they went back into the house a shadow slipped past them in the dusk, and the cat was there, wailing from a safe distance by the porch.

'Feed that one, you'll end up with half a dozen,' Gareth warned her, but Patsy could not resist the plaintive cries, and she gave the cat the rest of the stewed steak. The tabby gobbled it before vanishing again into the bushes, and Patsy offered Gareth a cup of tea.

Settled by the still glowing Rayburn, a steaming cup in his hand, Gareth looked round the room and at Patsy, tired and dishevelled in the other chair.

'You don't mind if I ask a question?' he said. 'Mam didn't like to, but you needn't answer. Why did you come? It can be lonely here, especially with you being English, not that it's something that worries us, although there is a few it will. Then there's the weather...we get days when you can hardly stand straight for the wind. There's times when the wet on the land breaks your heart, especially when the lambing's started, or the hay's set.'

'I'd always dreamed of a home like this,' Patsy tried to explain. 'Land of my own, beautiful country, away from suburban life. You say it can be lonely here, but I never fitted in too well in Surrey...struggling to keep my horses in a rented bit of land. I was never one for shopping and dinner parties, and for years my husband was ill and reliant. I never had time or space to myself. I've spent holidays round here, and when my husband died and I saw this place advertised, I couldn't resist coming to look. And once I'd looked, I just thought, why not? So here I am. Daughter thinks I'm mad...she's convinced I shall come to a bad end.'

'Or a good one,' said Gareth quietly. 'The farming's too hard... I've told my Dad that, it wasn't for me, but I'd still not want to live anywhere else. There's a special quality about this land...a magic, so it's said. Once it gets to you you don't want to leave.'

'Yes,' agreed Patsy, surprised. 'That's just how I feel about it. There are so many contrasts, and the light changes all the time...you feel that there could be another world brushing shoulders with you...that you might break through at any moment.'

'Especially when the wind's wild, and the tide's high, or the mist hangs on the hills, just shifting to let a ghost of the sun filter through.' Gareth laughed. 'That's quite poetic we're getting. Time I was off home to my tea. If you need more help, just call...and good luck.'

Patsy opened the door to let him out and then stood in the porch for a moment after he had driven away. Above the night sky was a mass of brilliant stars, the clouds having cleared away as the darkness came, and a shooting star streaked down the curved bowl of the night and vanished. Taking it as a good sign, Patsy closed the door and went to find herself some supper.

CHAPTER TWO

Sometime in the depths of the night Patsy was woken by a furious squalling from outside...the shrieks of an enraged cat, and hissing from something else. Switching on the light, Patsy went to the window and opened it. Light spilled out across the little garden and the edge of the yard below, and there was a bump and scuffle from somewhere and an enquiring roar from Goliath. Leaning out, Patsy clapped her hands hard, and then listened. There was silence except for the horses stirring in their stables.

'Fox,' decided Patsy, closing the window and returning to bed. 'Hope the cat's all right...nice little creature.'

She slept again, and when she went down and opened the back door next morning the cat was there, waiting. To her surprise, instead of waiting at a safe distance, the cat streaked in and seemed to be searching, sniffing urgently in corners, and seeming especially interested in the dark brick alcoves on either side of the stove, which Patsy had been glad to find still alight.

'Hey, do you want breakfast?' Patsy asked the cat. At the sound of her voice it seemed to remember where it was, and shot back out of the door again, where it turned to wait with the usual hopeful wail. Smiling, Patsy opened her last tin of stewed steak. She would have to find a shop later, and stock up with cat food...and human food and sometime she must buy a secondhand car...or rather, a fifth or sixth-hand one. She couldn't do all journeys in the Transit. The diesel for it would cost too much, quite apart from the awkwardness of manoeuvring it in tight corners and car parks.

It was a bright morning, with the soft feel of approaching spring: a perfect morning to introduce Goliath to riding in Pembrokeshire, Patsy decided.

Goliath was very doubtful about this venture. It meant leaving David behind at the mercy of still unknown perils, and it also meant relying on himself and his rider to avoid the strange bogeys that might be lurking out there. He made his way along the track from Patsy's cattle grid to the road staring and snorting, starting violently at every bird in the hedgerow and every white stone on the bank.

'You are an idiot,' Patsy told him, as she urged him forward. She was well used to his ways after twelve years. Jumping with Katy in her horsey days Goliath had been as brave as a lion, but jumps were things he understood. Strange lanes and even stranger hill country were not.

A short distance along the lane, a track, partly made up with two concrete strips either side of a grass strip, led towards the hills. High banks bounded it, starred already with primroses, and scattered with drifts of snowdrops, the start of the wild flower season: one of Pembrokeshire's glories. There were occasional gates along the lane, breaks in the banks at which Goliath shied violently in case something should be waiting to jump out at him,. A group of black cattle gathered round a feeder occupied by a large round bale of hay sent him scurrying almost up the opposite bank, and a buzzard rising lazily from a catch under the hedge caused a sudden, snorting stop.

'For goodness sake,' Patsy said to him. 'I'm not scared...why should you be?'

Goliath was not convinced, but they made it to a cattle grid with a gate beside it which led to a green, with one or two cottages beside it, and the track carrying on past them, and onto the open moor. Goliath accepted this with suspicion but when the track petered out to a muddy passageway between two small fields and out onto the moor proper suddenly there was nothing that he understood any more. He was a southern horse, used to bridleways and roads, and this sudden almost trackless open expanse of bracken and gorse, bogs and water, with rocks that did not move and sheep that did spooked him completely. He stopped dead, sending out a frantic, roaring neigh for help, and tried to turn round.

'Don't be a fool,' Patsy told him. 'It's quite safe...walk on...'

At the feel of her heels pressing him to go forward Goliath began to go up and down on the spot like a yo-yo, his head high and his nostrils blown wide, uttering piercing snorts. With much persuasion from Patsy they did progress a little, the flat, boggy part of the moor opening out around them, crossed by more streams, partly hidden by the channels they had cut through the soft ground. There was a great feeling of space, the wide, wild land of the bogs stretching round and the great green hills beyond rearing into the arching sky. Patsy felt dwarfed, the cold breeze from the hills blew into her face, and the air sang with the sounds of running water and shushing wind. There was also the sound of the harsh croaks of two crows picking at the almost skeleton carcase of a sheep beside a gorse bush. This last sight was too much for Goliath. Ignoring all Patsy's aids of hands, legs, and voice he span round and made a desperate attempt to charge back to the comparative familiarity of the green, the made-up track, and the cottages. The sight of a quad bike speeding towards them bouncing over the mud, driven by a boy in blue overalls with a black and white sheepdog perched on the carrier behind him, brought him to another abrupt stop. The bike stopped too, and the sheepdog leaped down and circled to come up behind Goliath, belly close to the ground, yellow eyes fixed on the horse as if it were a sheep. Goliath eyed it anxiously and let out another of his snorts. The boy on the bike laughed.

'Playing you up, is it?' he asked. 'Shall I tell the dog send him on?'

'No, it's all right,' Patsy was not thrilled by the idea of being herded willy-nilly onto the moor by a dog. 'It's all a bit too strange for him...I'll take him home and bring his friend with him next time.'

David would cope with the moor...he was a moorland pony himself, from Exmoor.

'Right,' said the boy. 'You'll be the new lady from Emrys's old place... Mrs. Evans was telling my Mam you're there all alone.'

'At the moment,' admitted Patsy. 'But I expect my daughter will visit...and other people.'

She was beginning to feel that too much discussion of her lone state might not be a good thing... she wanted to build a life for herself here...and not one founded on pity. She did not need pity, she was living a life-long dream...even if doing it alone.

'Fair play,' said the boy. 'I'll be getting on, then. There's a few sheep gone missing...not meant to be out here yet, they're not. Cap...up lad.'

The bike moved off, making a wide swerve round the snorting Goliath, the sheepdog leaping back onto his place on the carrier as it passed him. Patsy loosened the reins and let Goliath have his heart's desire...to trot as fast as possible home to David, and safety. It might be bad discipline but Patsy knew that Goliath was not being deliberately naughty, and his many years with her and Katy had earned him leniency.

'We'll come out again, with David, and sort out your horrors,' she told Goliath, as he power-walked back into the yard, roaring for David.

As Goliath came to a halt and deflated back to his normal size, Patsy saw a strange animal on top of the stone bank by the field gate. It was a long, ferret-like creature, only stockier, and with thick brown fur on top of its body and creamy fur beneath. It stared at her, bounced up and down rather like an angry cat at a mouse hole, and then turned and vanished into the field. As she dismounted Patsy saw the cat crouching in the barn doorway, every hair fluffed out and her tail like a bottle brush. At the sight of Patsy on foot she turned and vanished into the shadows behind her.

'Well, whatever was that thing?' Patsy asked Goliath, but he was only interested in rushing up to David's stable and thrusting his head inside to make sure that the brown head watching him really did belong to his dear friend and protector. Gently removing him, Patsy took him into his own stable to unsaddle him.

She was taking her boots off in the porch a few minutes later when the cat slid past her and into the house with something in her mouth.

'No!' Patsy hobbled after her with one boot still on. 'I don't want a mouse...'

She followed the cat into the living room just in time to see her emerge from one of the brick alcoves beside the stove. There was no longer anything in her mouth, but from the deep shadows of the alcove came a high, plaintive squeak. A kitten. The cat stared at Patsy, tail low, yellow eyes fixed on Patsy's face. Quite clearly she was asking if it was all right.

'So is that what all the noise was about in the night?' Patsy asked her. 'Something was after your kitten...that something that was on the bank just now.'

The cat continued to stare at her, and Patsy backed away a little.

'All right,' she said. 'It can stay...and so can you. I'll get you some food...then it looks as if I'll have to go shopping.'

She finished pulling off her boot, and she was in the kitchen getting the tin of sardines...no stewed steak left now...when the cat came back into the house with another kitten dangling from her mouth.

'How many more?' Patsy asked. She stayed where she was, watching. The cat made one more trip...three kittens in safety in the alcove. Then she came up to Patsy, looking up at the tin in her hand, and gave her usual pleading wail.

'I can see you're going to cost me a fortune in cat food,' Patsy told her, as she set the dish of sardines in front of the cat and watched the voracious appetite at work. 'The sooner I get you something cheaper than stewed steak and sardines the better.'

The nearest shopping town of any size was Cardigan, or Aberteifi, to give it its Welsh name. There was a large Tesco supermarket on the bypass, and Patsy decided to visit that, in spite of a guilty feeling that by doing so, and not supporting the smaller in-town traders, she was going for the best from two worlds. It seemed, however, that she was not the only one. The large car park was almost full, and Patsy's Transit was not out of place. There was a cattle lorry and another small horse box, as well as numerous four wheel drives in varying states of mud, several with metal cattle trailers attached. There was even a tractor in one corner, towering over the ordinary cars.

After trawling round the store, collecting as many useful supplies as she could think of, Patsy was lining up at the check-out when she felt a touch on her sleeve, and Rhiannon's voice said, 'So you found the way to the shoppers' paradise, then?'

'Yes, and it's just like the one back in England,' Patsy told her. 'There was me imagining shopping at some luscious rural market, and here I am, back in Tesco.'

'Like the rest of us,' said Rhiannon, eyeing the cat food. 'Found yourself a pet, I see, Gareth said there was a cat begging. I expect Emrys used to feed it, never could resist an animal begging, could he now. Still, fair play, he did get on best with the animals.'

Patsy told her about the kittens, and the creature on the wall, and Rhiannon nodded.

'That'd be a polecat,' she said. 'Nasty, vicious things, they're making quite a come back round here. They will take kittens, and not even the new young lambs are safe. Worse than foxes, they are.'

Once through the check-out they pushed their laden carts towards the waiting rows of cars. There was a sheep trailer attached to the back of Rhiannon's old Land Rover, and Rhiannon said, 'It's back to the market for me, now, see how John's been getting on selling five old ewes. They won't have made much more than the cost of getting them down here, I shouldn't wonder.'

'That bad, is it?' asked Patsy, and Rhiannon sighed.

'Not much better,' she said. 'Our Gareth's maybe not so daft, getting out of the farming. John and me are meeting him and his girl friend, Bethan, for a bite of lunch: he's in Cardigan today seeing someone about software. Now that was something I'd once have thought was pillows, but I've had to learn better to tackle the farm paperwork.'

Patsy laughed, and Rhiannon stopped to open the door of her Land Rover. 'Have a nice lunch,' Patsy wished her.

Walking on, she could not help thinking how nice it must be to have a satisfactory son like Gareth, who settled for a nice, no doubt 'decent' girl friend, instead of her own daughter's doubtful attachment to her flighty married man. It wouldn't matter so much if Andrew made Katy happy, but all the relationship seemed to do was keep Katy on a constant wire of stress and uncertainty.

The sun was fading as Patsy drove home, hidden by a rising, swift-moving bank of cloud. Driving along the high road from Cardigan she could see the mist dropping like a blanket, already hiding the hills, and by the time she turned into her lane it was raining, a thick drizzle blown on a rising wind from the west. The horses were at the gate, Goliath hunched and miserable, plainly complaining that he had been left out in the rain, unloved, for hours, and David cheerfully nibbling the hedge. There was a welcoming warmth coming from the Rayburn, Patsy was glad to feel, and the cat peered at her, eyes gleaming green from the dark safety of her alcove, her kittens pressed against her soft stomach. Patsy carried her bags inside, and began storing them away, and soon became aware that she was being watched. The cat was in the doorway, and when she knew that Patsy had seen her she opened her mouth in a silent meow.

'I think if you and I are going to live together it's time we got a bit closer,' Patsy told her. 'If you want food you'll have to let me touch you first.'

She crouched down, and the cat backed off, still staring.

'You could be a beautiful puss if you got a bit fatter,' Patsy told her, in her 'cat wheedling' voice. 'Beautiful lady...come on then...come and talk...'

The cat's fixed gaze shifted, dropped, and then focussed again, but to one side of Patsy. A sudden cold prickle ran down Patsy's back. It was almost as if the cat was looking at someone else...resisting the urge to look round Patsy kept her hand out, and the cat came a hesitant step nearer. She just allowed Patsy to touch her head, and then she suddenly fluffed up, her tail grew large, and she was gone, back to the kittens, and the safety of the alcove. Patsy stood up slowly, aware that the kitchen was very cold, and conscious of a feeling that she was not alone. It was an effort to turn round, but Patsy did so, her skin prickling. There was nothing there.

'It was that cat,' she decided determinedly. 'She was spooked by me, and it gave me the creeps.'

She took one of the tins of cat food from the shelf, and began to open it. At the sound, and the rattle of a spoon, the cat came creeping back, and this time she settled down to eat with her usual gusto. When she had finished, Patsy crouched down, and held out a hand, and this time the cat came cautiously up to sniff it, and then relaxed enough to let Patsy stroke her head.

'You'll do,' Patsy told her. 'We'll get along well enough, I'm sure.'

The kitchen had become very dark, and looking out of the window, Patsy saw veils of rain sweeping across the fields. She could see Goliath, pressed to the gate, and she decided to take pity on him and bring both horses into their stables.

It had turned much colder with the rain and wind, and the yard was very bleak, water running down it, down the gentle slope on which the whole property was set. The house, from David's stable, looked dark and withdrawn, set against the weather as it had been for the last hundred years. There were jackdaws huddled together against the warm chimney from the stove, and a buzzard, heading for the shelter of the woods behind the house, floated low overhead, giving its wild, cat-like cry. Patsy shivered and turned back to the friendly, familiar warmth of the kind old pony. She would not let herself dwell on the idea that perhaps she had made a stupid mistake in coming here. If only Katy had still been beside her, sharing the horses and the outdoors, the fun and effort, as she had until Andrew had walked into her life. But she had to accept the fact that Katy, like all daughters, had grown up and away.

'It's up to me now,' Patsy told herself. 'I may be a bit old for this, but I'm going to give it my best.'

It rained for the rest of the afternoon and through the evening. Indoors the wind banged the badly fitting porch door, and whined down the chimneys. Patsy went to bed early, tired, and trying not to let in the depression that she could feel hovering.

She was woken suddenly by a loud bang. Sitting up in bed, Patsy switched on her bedside lamp, and at the same moment a gust of wind swooshed through the room, lifting the curtains and sending objects flying off the dressing table. Patsy realised that her window was wide open. Staggering out of bed she pulled the curtains aside and leaned out into the wind and rain. The top half of the window was built on a swivel, and it had lifted right up. Patsy had to hang right out to reach it and pull it down. She had done it, her head and shoulders soaked, and was securing the latch, when the bedside lamp suddenly went out, leaving the room in total darkness. Patsy swung round, her back to the window, and at the same time she heard another window slam open on the landing.

For a moment, completely disorientated, Patsy could not remember which way led to the light switch. The room had become bitterly cold, with the wet air from outside, and something else, something that was chilling the air even more as Patsy felt her way along the wall to the switch. Finding it, she pressed it down, but nothing happened: the room remained dark. Her torch was downstairs, Patsy knew, left near the back door in case of outdoor emergencies. The strange stairs, in the pitch dark, were not an inviting prospect, but neither was remaining in this thick, inky blackness. Standing there, Patsy began to make out a glimmer of light in the windows, and she could just make out the shape of the top banister. There was nothing for it but to feel her way down to the torch, and the trip-switches. It had to be something simple like that: a blown bulb in the bedside lamp would have been enough to throw the switch.

Slowly, step by step, Patsy made her way down and along the hall into the back room. The switches were in a box above her head in the alcove by the back door. Finding her torch upended on the shelf by the door Patsy switched it on. Sure enough, one of the switches was down. Patsy carried a chair across, and climbed on it to push the switch back, and to her relief she saw the glow from upstairs as the bedroom light came back on.

'Sorted.' Patsy relaxed. Nothing strange, after all. Switching on the lights as she went, Patsy made her way back up the stairs. The window was still wide open, and again she had to lean right out into the wet wind to pull it shut. She was securing it when the bathroom window crashed open, and there was another crash as something blew off the shelf in there.

'No!' Patsy could not stop her sudden cry. 'Stop it...'

There was a sudden feeling of stillness: even the draught through the open window seemed to stop for a moment. Then the wind gusted in again, and Patsy went to cope with the third window. That closed, she stopped, and turned to face the room. It looked completely normal. A jar of bath salts, dislodged from the shelf, was the only sign that anything had happened.

'Is that it?' Patsy asked the empty air, but all remained still. Whatever had caused the windows to open had stopped.

'It was the wind,' Patsy told herself firmly. 'You will not start scaring yourself in the middle of the night.' A cup of tea and a dry night-shirt were the obvious solutions.

The dry night-shirt came first. Coming back onto the landing a few minutes later, wearing a warm dressing gown, Patsy was aware of a strange draught blowing down on her from above. Looking up, she felt the first real, deep shiver of primeval fear run down her body. The hatch into the attic was open, a dark, gaping hole in the ceiling.

'A an up-draught...from the open windows.' Patsy hung back by her bedroom door, holding herself tight, knowing that she was only inches away from panic. She was being watched...she was sure of it...but from where...and by what?

Fighting the urge to dive back into her room and slam the door, Patsy forced herself to go along the landing. The square hole was directly above her: there was no loft ladder, and the only way up was from a stepladder, or a chair, if she could reach. There was a chair in one of the spare rooms...Patsy fetched it, and a torch, and with every nerve prickling she stepped up onto it, stood on tip-toe, and shone the torch into the wide, black space under the roof. The beam of her torch showed a couple of dusty tea chests, the slope of the roof, and the faint gleam of insulating material spread over the ceiling joists. There was nowhere for anyone to hide: even lying flat against the eaves Patsy knew she would have seen them. The hatch cover was tipped back to one side, and with a great stretch Patsy got hold of the edge, and pulled it over her head. It dropped into its space with a substantial thud, and when she pushed it Patsy found that it was quite a firm fit.

'It was still the wind,' Patsy said out loud. 'I must not imagine things.'

Turning, she only just managed not to scream. There was something at the top of the stairs, a shadow with twin green lights in the centre....almost at once Patsy knew it was the cat.

'Puss...' Patsy's voice shook. 'What...what are you doing up here...?'

'That proves there isn't a ghost,' she was thinking, but then she remembered Rhiannon saying that Emrys used to feed her. Perhaps that would mean the cat had no fear of her old friend...Patsy stopped herself.

The cat had heard her moving, and been disturbed by the draught; she was probably after more food.

'All right, I'll have a cup of tea, and you can have some food,' Patsy told her, and, switching on every light as she passed the switches, Patsy followed the cat into the kitchen.

Nothing else happened that night, and Patsy woke to find it still raining and blowing outside. There were seagulls in the field, a scattering of white, searching for food in some shelter from the wind. Struggling to carry hay across the yard to the stables without having it blown out of her arms, Patsy wondered again if she really was mad to come here. Then during breakfast, a sudden shaft of sunlight fell across the table, and looking out, Patsy saw that the clouds were sweeping away, leaving behind a clear washed pale-blue sky patched with flying clumps of white cloud. Everything sparkled and Patsy decided that the best way to clear her head after her restless night was to saddle Goliath, put David on the leading rein, and test all their nerves on the mountain.

With David at his side Goliath was much braver. They reached the cattle grid and the gate onto the green with no more than several snorts. David, well used to going out like this since Katy had given up riding and left Patsy with them both, trotted at his companion's shoulder, ears pricked, wise eyes bright with interest under his thick forelock. An Exmoor pony, the open wilderness in front of them did not worry him. They passed the sheep pens and came to a stream, deeply undercutting overhanging banks thick with gorse, but with one wide, clear crossing place. The water looked quite deep, stained brown from the peat higher up, and racing over rocks and stones to flow under a single plank bridge, much too narrow and slippery for horses.

'Time to get your feet wet,' Patsy told her two, as Goliath hesitated, snorting, on the brink. David was all eagerness, head down to nose the cold water, and Patsy let the leading rein out to its full length. With David slightly ahead to lead the way Goliath gingerly set one foot in the water, and decided that it was safe. Beyond it Patsy saw a stony track, like a causeway, built up above the level of the boggy ground, leading directly towards the hills and a group of bright green, enclosed fields on the first upward slope, with what looked like the ruins of a small farm in the centre. There was water everywhere, pouring in narrow streaks down the hillside and clattering over the stones beside the track. Two buzzards floated overhead, and large crows perched, croaking to each other, on the bare, scrubby thorn bushes which dotted the flat land. As they passed the ruined farm, the made-up track ended, and only a sheep path led on upwards. Soon both horses were puffing, especially Goliath, and Patsy took pity on them and turned them to stand while she looked at the view.

All around now the hills rose bare and silent towards the great, arching sky. White clouds drew swift shadows across their slopes, and back the way that they had come lay a patchwork of the lower moor, and beyond that small fields and white homesteads, with beyond it all a glimpse of the sea, blue and shimmering in the frame made by the hills. The silence was tangible, broken only by the mewing of the buzzards and the deep breathing of the horses. Patsy was about to ride on when there was a vibration in the air, a faint, unearthly shriek. She just had time to see the black V shape of the approaching Air Force jet, just skimming the hills, every detail of the undercarriage clear as it swept above them, before the shattering scream of its engines, trailing behind, broke over them. Both horses leaped forward in alarm: even David startled, his ears flat, while Goliath was off up the hill with his head in the air, and David's leading rein was snatched out of Patsy's hand.

'Steady, it's all right, whoa, Golly.' Patsy tugged at Goliath's mouth, but already the steepness of the hill was stopping him. Patsy had him almost back under control when the scream of a second jet, slightly more distant, sent him off again. This time his scare ended more quickly; already he was recognising the noise as man-made, like the traffic he was used to, and eventually less scary than this open country. Hauling him to a stop Patsy looked round for David.

The smaller pony had decided to explore. He was trotting off at an angle to the sheep path, through a patch of dead bracken which grew up the hillside, and Patsy saw a group of moorland ponies ahead of him, turning to stare at the stranger coming towards them. Goliath saw them too, and saw his departing friend, and with one of his desperate roars he began to leap up and down in his usual yo-yo fashion.

'David,' shouted Patsy. 'David...come on...'

David took no notice. He was intent on investigating these interesting strangers. Patsy was beginning to panic, visualising David joining with the herd and herself stranded out here with a hysterical Goliath, when she saw a large white horse with a black head and mane coming round the shoulder of the hill from the other direction at a canter. There was a man on its back, riding with loose reins, apparently careless of the rough ground.

'Stay there,' he shouted to Patsy. 'Don't worry, I'll get him'

David had stopped, head up, staring at the newcomer, and the herd was scattering into the bracken. Before David had time to think of following them, the big horse was alongside, and its rider hung onto the mane with one hand while he leaned down to grab David's trailing rein with the other.

'OK, got him,' he shouted, and came on at a trot, a startled David scurrying at his side.

Goliath was cantering on the spot, snorting with alarm and excitement, as the big horse skated to a stop beside them. The rider, Patsy saw, was quite an elderly man, with a hollow cheeked, weather-beaten face and strands of greying hair showing under his very faded riding hat. Hauling his horse round he handed David's rein to Patsy. With his friend back beside him Goliath subsided, and the two sniffed noses and tossed their heads, David bright-eyed after his adventure.

'Thank you.' Patsy felt limp with relief. 'I'd never have got him back without your help, not today, anyway.'

'Thank Osbourne,' replied the man. 'He saw your chap coming, and decided to join in. I just grabbed him in passing. Name's Mackintosh, by the way, Everard Mackintosh. Normally I answer to "Mack."'

'Patricia Heath,' Patsy replied. 'I answer to "Patsy."'

'And you're at old Jones's place,' said Mack, who was now sitting on his horse with the reins loose on its neck, while he lit a cigarette. 'My wife has you on her list for an invite to dinner.'

'That's very kind of her.' Patsy was again taken by surprise by the realisation that everyone knew who she was.

'Not that kind,' Mack had his cigarette going by now. 'Pure curiosity, I'm afraid. It's not long since a new English face in the district was quite a thrill; lots more coming in now, of course, but it still makes for a change. Hope you don't mind?'

'Oh, I'm quite happy to be a change,' Patsy assured him. 'I need to get to know people as much as they seem to know me, anyway.'

'Good point,' agreed Mack. 'Our place is at the end of the village, next to the bridge on the B road, Glyn Afon. Come tomorrow night, about seven...right?'

'Thank you.' Patsy was pleased. 'I'd like to.'

'Are you going on up?' Mack asked her. 'Osbourne and I are heading home now, but we'd be glad to show you the way round another time. Bit tricky in places, lots of bogs.'

'I think we've had enough for one morning as well,' Patsy told him. 'But I'd be glad of a guide one day.'

'Right.' Mack gathered up his reins, and Osbourne, who had been sniffing at the short, rough grass under his feet, moved off. Goliath was only too pleased to follow, and David jogged alongside, ears pricked, pleased with himself after his adventure.

As they dropped down from the hill the track levelled out, and without warning Mack gave Osbourne a kick, and the big black and white horse broke into a canter. Patsy had no time to shorten her reins and get hold of Goliath, and she found herself thundering in pursuit, David, thrilled, pulling at his lead rein for all he was worth. The ground was rough, and the ride fast and bumpy, and by the time they reached the sheep pens and Mack pulled up, so quickly that Goliath almost ran into him, Patsy was breathless, with aching arms.

'Short cut here for us,' Mack said, over his shoulder. 'Through the back of the farm...you carry straight on. Next time I'll take you over the top. Seven tomorrow...goodbye.'

He turned Osbourne into a narrow path which skirted the pens, and Patsy, after a short argument with Goliath, who wanted to go that way as well, rode on. Over the top with Mack would need some thinking about if he always rode at that speed.

After the wildness of the mountain, and the mild adventure, it felt good to be arriving home. Patsy was feeling peaceful and ready for lunch as they came round the bend, and she saw her entrance in front of them, She was surprised to see that the gate beside the cattle grid was closed, having been sure that she had left it open when they set out. Now she would have to get off to open it: it was too difficult to do with two horses.

On foot, Goliath's reins over her arm and David's rein in her hand, Patsy pulled back the latch and pushed. Nothing happened. The latch would not disengage. Patsy tried pushing harder, and lifting the gate, but still with no success. Goliath was becoming impatient, pushing the gate with his nose, and pawing at the ground with one large front foot.

'This is ridiculous,' said Patsy, aloud. 'It's always opened easily enough up to now.'

She pushed, lifted, and eventually kicked the gate, but still with no success. The horses were becoming increasingly impatient, Goliath was starting to eye the cattle grid, and Patsy began to be afraid that he would try to barge across it, and get his legs caught. Goliath was not used to cattle grids, although David probably remembered them from his youth on Exmoor. There was no other way into her home from here, and Patsy knew that there was no mobile signal from her new home. She remembered how easily Goliath had made his way into Rhiannon's land on their first evening. They would have to try that. Crossly, Patsy remounted, turned the very unwilling horses round, and set off back up her lane to the turning which led to the Evans's farm.

Rhiannon's house was a larger version of Patsy's, half a width longer, stone-built, with a very tidy farmyard beside it. Some cattle stared at Patsy and the horses from an open-fronted barn, and there were a few sheep in an enclosed yard to one side. At the sound of hooves the two collies came swiftly and silently to meet her, and a man followed them from behind the cattle barn, a short, stocky man with greying hair and the quiet, lined face that Patsy had noticed was typical of the local farmers, a look that came from a lifetime of living in this isolated area, battling with the weather and quietly confident of their place in their community, and their country.

'Er...hello...?' Patsy was about to explain herself when Rhiannon's voice behind her said, 'Well, come visiting and brought your friends, I see. John, this is Mrs Heath from Emrys's place.'

'How are you?' John Evans did not smile, but the nod he gave Patsy was friendly enough.

'Fine, thank you,' said Patsy. 'I'm glad to meet you. The only thing is, I've got a bit of a problem.'

She explained about the gate, and saw John and Rhiannon exchange a quick glance. Then John said, 'I'll come on back with you, then, and try what I can do. Wait now, while I get the Land Rover.'

'I'm sorry to be a nuisance,' said Patsy, but John was already turning towards his vehicle, and Rhiannon patted Goliath's neck.

'No problem,' she said. 'John won't mind helping. I think you'll find it's no big job he'll have with it.'

John was climbing into the Land Rover, and as Patsy turned her horses back to the gate he drove out ahead of her. In spite of the speed at which Goliath insisted on trotting now that his nose was again towards home, by the time they reached it John already had the gate open, and he was standing in the yard beside his Land Rover.

'Oh, thank you.' Patsy stopped the horses beside him. 'What was wrong with it?'

'Not a thing.' John told her. 'Opened at a touch.'

'How odd.' Patsy stared at him, and John smiled, a smile which lit up his eyes, and transformed his whole face. Patsy had a glimpse of the lively young man whom Rhiannon had married.

'It is that,' he agreed. 'Almost as if someone was having fun with you, isn't it now? Well, I'd best get back to my cows. Any more problems, give us a call. This is your home now, you remember that, girl.'

Still smiling he got back into the Land Rover, swung it round in a tight circle, and rattled away over the cattle grid, leaving Patsy staring after him.

'Someone having fun with me?' she thought, as she dismounted. 'But is it fun...or is it more serious?'

The horses out in their field, Patsy let herself into the house. The cat ran to meet her, complaining that she was being starved, and that it was cold for her kittens, and Patsy knew at once from the feel of the room that the stove had gone out again. Sighing, she fetched newspaper and kindling and started once more on the laborious task of re-lighting it. As she had expected, all of the dampers which she had left nicely adjusted were closed tight.

'Why?' she asked the still air of the room. 'Is it just fun? Or don't you like me being here? Do you want the house to stay empty...fall down? No-one else was queuing up to buy it.'

Of course, there was no reply, but for a moment, as she sat back on her heels and reached for the matches, Patsy had a feeling that someone was listening.

CHAPTER THREE

The stove lighted quite easily, and with it roaring away Patsy went into the kitchen to open a tin of soup and cut some bread for her lunch. While she was eating, the patch of sunlight faded from the wall beside her and soon it was raining again, a soft, clinging drizzle which blotted out the hills and blew in thick waves across the fields. Patsy took her coffee into the front room and switched on the television to watch the lunchtime news, and before long she had drifted off to sleep. She was woken some time later by the rising wind banging something up in the loft.

Getting up from her chair, Patsy stretched limbs stiff from the morning's ride, and thought ruefully that not so long ago she would not have stiffened up like this. There was no escaping the fact that at sixty she was less supple than she used to be, even if inside she felt no different. There had always been a deep inner core to her, something neither changed nor really satisfied by marriage, one daughter and the death of her other baby soon after birth, her husband's long history of illness and mental problems, or any of the other events and traumas of life. This move to Wales, which Katy found so hard to understand, was brought about by that core, the part of her that found ultimate satisfaction in the outdoors, the horses, and, up to a point, the isolation and aloneness of her new life.

The banging in the loft needed investigating. Rather reluctantly Patsy fetched the step ladder from the outhouse by the back door and carried it upstairs. The loft trapdoor was still in place, she was relieved to see, and when she lifted it back there was no bogey waiting on the other side, and her torch showed the source of the banging. A loose piece of board laid over the joists was lifting up and down on the draught blowing under the eaves. Patsy moved it forward, and heaved across one of the dusty tea chests that had been left up there so that the board was weighted down. Then, curious to see what had been left behind, she shone her torch into the box. Packs of magazines, old *Farmers Weeklies* and some other papers in Welsh, old copies of *Horse and Hound*, and some more Welsh magazines with pictures of the Welsh pony breeds in them. Some of these were sufficiently old to be worth a further look, and Patsy dropped them down through the trap door before turning to a smaller box with a lid. Inside were records of Emrys's successes with livestock at shows, old prize cards for cattle and ponies, rosettes and programmes for agricultural shows. Then, at the bottom, carefully wrapped in tissue, Patsy found two more rosettes, huge championship rosettes with the name 'Royal Welsh' stamped onto them in gold. The date on the blocked tails was ten years earlier. Impressed, Patsy gazed at them in the torch light.

'The Royal Welsh,' she said aloud. 'That really is something. I wonder what they were for?'

Sitting back on her heels she imagined the thrill, the packed stands and the ring crowded with...what? Ponies? Cobs? Cattle? Whatever it was the glory would be the same, a top award at Wales's premier show. There was something else in the box, this time wrapped in newspaper as well as tissue: a flat package, a framed photograph. Carefully Patsy unwrapped it. The picture was of a cob stallion, a chestnut, with a long, pale, flowing mane and tail, standing with head high and neck arched, his every hair bursting with pride and power, the two huge rosettes on his stallion bridle, and a large silvery cup on a small table beside him. The lead rein went out of the picture, so that he appeared to be standing alone, and the caption beneath read 'Bryn Uchaf Highflyer'.

'A cob stallion,' thought Patsy. 'What a beauty. But this should be downstairs, not hidden up here; even if the farm has changed hands, he was still a champion from here.'

Still holding the photograph and the rosettes, Patsy climbed down from the loft, then closed the trapdoor behind her. She would find a good place for them: the shelf above the alcove that contained the stove seemed a good spot.

Watched curiously by the cat, who was sitting outside the alcove, Patsy climbed onto a chair and carefully placed the photograph in the middle of the shelf. She pinned the rosettes on either side, and then got down and stood back to look. It was a good spot: the photograph seemed to dominate the room with the stallion's air of power and presence. Standing there, she was suddenly sure there was someone behind her, but when she swung round the room was empty. Patsy smiled to herself. Perhaps displaying his photograph would soften old Emrys up a bit. She had a mental vision of a typical local ancient farmer, stringy and bent from years out in the weather. No wonder he resented a soft Englishwoman coming to play at life in a place to which he had no doubt been a slave.

Patsy was heading for the door, about to go out into the rain and bring in her old horses, when there was a thud and a disturbance behind her. The cat streaked past, heading for the door with every hair on end, and Patsy span round to see the photograph and the rosettes lying on the floor while both oven doors swung open.

'What's this about?' Patsy's voice was shaky. 'I thought you'd like seeing that picture and your rosettes on display. I would, if they'd belonged to me.'

Around her the air seemed to vibrate with anger. Patsy's nerve almost broke. She wanted to run out of the door and hide in the field with the horses, but that was no good. Whatever this was, her own imagination or a ghost, she had to face it out.

'All right,' she said. 'If you don't like it I'll put them back...will that do? Next time I decide to put a prize or a photo up there I'll make sure it's mine, and about something I've won myself.'

The air seemed to vibrate with silent, derisive laughter, and Patsy felt suddenly angry.

'Why shouldn't I win something?' she asked. 'I could show a pony as much as you did. Maybe I will.'

She pulled up a chair, climbed onto it, and removed the photograph and the rosettes. Going back into the dark loft swept her sudden anger away, leaving her cold, with the hairs prickling at the back of her neck, but nothing else happened. Patsy stowed the photo and the rosettes away in their box, climbed down, and returned nervously to the living room. The doors of the ovens still hung open, and the cat was investigating one of them. The vibrations were gone.

Patsy closed the oven doors, and the cat returned to her rapidly growing kittens. Patsy put on her outdoor clothes and went rather thankfully outside into the rain to fetch the horses in. It was very therapeutic, rubbing them down, and feeding and haying them, Patsy gave Goliath a final pat and let herself out of his stable ready to go indoors. Turning from bolting it she froze. There was someone watching her, out there in the wet dusk, standing in the middle of the yard on the fringe of the rain blurred light from the yard lamps. Patsy could make out a short, stocky, powerful figure wearing dark clothes and a cap. Then a powerful gust of wind drove a wave of thicker rain across the yard and when it cleared the figure was gone.

'It's nonsense,' Patsy told herself. 'I'm getting spooked about nothing; there can't possibly be a ghost.'

She was hesitating there when the telephone began to ring, the outside bell sounding stridently through the rain. Determinedly Patsy went indoors to answer it.

'Mum? You took ages to answer, are you all right?' Katy sounded quite concerned.

'Yes, I'm fine, I was outside, putting the boys to bed,' Patsy told her, aware that her voice sounded a little high and strained. Katy noticed it too.

'Are you sure nothing's happened?' she asked. 'You sound a bit odd.'

So would you if you thought you'd just seen a ghost, thought Patsy, but she was not going to tell Katy about that. 'I'm just out of breath,' she said now. 'I rushed in to answer the 'phone. How are things with you? How's Andrew?'

Andrew was the stressful boy friend, still being stressful, by the sound of Katy's reply.

'He's got to go away, to a funeral, he says.' Katy sounded stressed herself. 'He...he says he's got to take Amanda with him, so I have to keep out of the way.'

'Well, if it's a family funeral, perhaps she'll be expected.' Patsy tried to defuse the situation, Amanda being Andrew's supposedly estranged wife. 'Why don't you come down here, visit and see my new home?'

'I...I suppose I could.' Katy sounded doubtful. 'But he says he'll only be gone a couple of days. I...I might stay around.'

'Katy,' Patsy decided to say what she felt. 'If Andrew is serious about you it wouldn't matter if you were to come here for a month, he'd still be waiting and if he wasn't, well, at least you'd know.'

'I couldn't do that anyway.' Katy, as usual, avoided the issue. 'I couldn't stay off work; I'd loose my job.'

Katy worked at the reception desk of a large hospital, which was where she had met Andrew, a physiotherapist.

'Oh, I know, I was just making a point,' Patsy told her. 'But a weekend...'

She didn't want to beg, but the thought of having Katy around, interested, lively, and young, was suddenly rather inviting.

'I'll think about it. I suppose I ought to come and see where it is that you've buried yourself.' Katy sounded quite interested, but Patsy knew that she would never commit herself unless she felt confident about what Andrew would be up to. Soon she rang off, and Patsy turned back to face her ghost. But the house was calm, the stove burning warmly, the cat and her family asleep. Relieved, Patsy went to get herself some supper.

The following day was peaceful. There were no strange happenings, and Patsy spent the day sorting out her belongings into final order, and looking after the horses. By evening, when it was time to get ready for her outing to eat with Mack and his wife, Patsy was beginning to relax again.

Patsy dressed carefully in loose black trousers and a peacock blue silk tunic. It seemed to be a long time since she had dressed up for anything; her husband had not been one for social outings, especially as he grew older and more unwell. As she still had no transport apart from the horse box she had to go in that, hoping that there would be a safe space in which to park it when she got there.

Mack's house was a modern bungalow, but not a local, run-of-the-mill estate design. It was long and interesting, L-shaped, and set in a garden which Patsy could see, even in the dusk, was beautifully laid out and kept. Spring flowers glowed in the borders, early flowering shrubs were in bloom, and a great bush of forsythia glowed like trapped sunlight in a corner by the house. There was space to leave the horse box in a stony track which led past the house towards the moor gate and Patsy, feeling rather nervous, made her way up the gravel path to the front door.

Mack opened the door himself, casual but smart in well-pressed grey trousers and a navy cashmere sweater over a blue checked shirt. Without his hat his hair was white, smooth, and quite long, and Patsy could see that he was quite elderly, in spite of his dashing riding. There was a good smell of roasting meat, and the entrance hall, with its blue and red carpet and white paint, was warm and welcoming.

'Come in, come and have a drink.' Mack led the way and opened a door into the living room. An impression of comfortable living greeted Patsy: a deep, pale apricot carpet, apricot and white paint, deep, comfortable armchairs and a huge white settee. There was a shining black metal log burner stove sending out waves of heat, and a great glass vase of daffodils, forsythia, and tulips stood on a polished table in front of the window, Heavy dark gold curtains were drawn across the glass, and bookshelves lined one of the walls. It was worlds away from the traditional farm house decor of most of the houses Patsy had visited in Wales. Mack went across to a well-stocked drink cabinet.

'What will you drink?' he asked. 'Plenty of choice...sherry, gin, whisky...?'

'Sherry please.' Patsy heard the door open behind her, and turned to meet Mack's wife.

'Tabitha, this is Patsy Heath.' Mack made the introductions. 'My wife, Tabitha, Tabby Cat, she tends to be called.'

'By my dear husband,' retorted Tabitha. 'I'm so pleased to meet you. The whole district has been agog with news of the brave lady who has come to live alone at Emrys Jones's old house.'

'Well...it's nice to give people some fun, I suppose.' Patsy felt immediately defensive. 'I must say it doesn't seem to need much bravery.'

Mack's wife could be well named, she suspected...there was something of the cat in her slight, supple figure and her slightly slanting greenish eyes in a small, pointed face. Her skin was crumpled, her hair, untouched by dye, was short and curly and streaked grey and brown, and there was slightly malicious fun in her smile.

'No ghosts, then?' she asked, startling Patsy. 'No sign of the old boy muttering Welsh curses in the chimney corner?'

'Er...' Patsy was trying to decide how to reply when Mack came to her rescue with a glass of sherry.

'Hang up a bit of garlic,' he said cheerfully. 'Gets rid of most ghosts...How's that cheeky pony of yours, then? Osbourne was quite taken with him.'

'He's fine...settling down, I hope.' Patsy was glad to have the subject changed, and yet she wondered just what stories there really were about Emrys. It would be nice to know, but she sensed that Tabitha would be only too pleased to add any information that Patsy gave her about him to the local fund of gossip.

Dinner, served in a dining room of polished period furniture, dark red carpet, and small, choice prints hung against the Regency-striped wallpaper, was a beautifully cooked and served meal of roast beef with all the trimmings, followed by a delicious home-made rice pudding. From her hosts Patsy learned a good deal about her neighbours, including Rhiannon's family.

'John Evans's family have farmed that place for generations,' Mack told her. 'Great disappointment to old John when the son decided farming wasn't for him. Rhiannon took it better, she's from the south, bit more of an urban outlook, you might say.'

'Yes, she taught John not to think that the English were guilty of every ill in Wales,' Tabitha put in. 'That never got through to Emrys, never did speak a word to us, only a grudging 'Bore Da' if we banged into him in the shop. He'll be spinning in his grave like a top, knowing one of the English is in his house.'

'How long have you lived here?' Patsy asked.

'Oh, must be fifteen years now.' Mack poured more wine into Patsy's glass, making her glad that she only had a short stretch of road to drive to get home. 'Since I retired...always had an eye on getting a place round here. So have a lot of the English...as you know.'

'One of the things we're accused of, of course,' said Tabitha. 'Turning Wales into a rest home for the geriatric English.'

'What brought you here, Patsy?' Mack asked her, and Patsy knew that she owed them a proper explanation.

'I'd wanted to get away from south-east England for years,' she said. 'But my husband didn't want to move...he'd taken early retirement from the Civil Service because his health was bad, but he felt secure in our home area. He'd only been dead a short time when I saw Bryn Uchaf advertised, and it just seemed meant...exactly the right time, a low price, and a good market for our old house. My daughter, Katy, thought it was a crazy idea, but she didn't want to come; she has her own life back in Surrey, and she'd rather left me with her two old horses. I was tired of trekking backwards and forwards to their rented field, and I was sick of the traffic and the crowding and being too close to the M25. So I took a deep breath and came. So far, I certainly haven't regretted it.'

'And I hope you won't,' Tabitha told her. 'Don't mind my stories: I'm sure your house is fine.'

'Of course it is,' said Mack, rather heartily. 'Now, let's go and sit down comfortably, and Tabby will make us some delicious coffee...'

Patsy enjoyed the rest of the evening. With Mack's guidance, Tabitha kept off the subject of Patsy's life and new home, and Patsy learned quite a lot about the rest of her new neighbours, the sometimes problems with the Welsh language, and things to do in the district.

'The theatre in Cardigan has been refurbished: it's well worth a visit now,' Mack told her. 'And something you should do is visit Llanbydder horse sales...last Thursday in each month.'

'If you don't mind being harrowed,' added Tabitha. 'I'm not a horse person, but some of the sights you see there...'

'It's improved a lot,' Mack told her. 'Better ruling on horse export and the care of them...'

'If the RSPCA catch up with the careless ones,' put in Tabitha.

'It's still worth a visit,' insisted Mack. 'Welsh life as it is lived...street market, trotting horses, and all.'

Patsy said that she would bear it in mind. At about eleven she felt that it was time to make a move for home, and after she had thanked Tabitha for the meal, Mack went with her to the door, and saw the Transit parked in the track.

'It's my only transport at the moment,' Patsy explained. 'I must find a small, sensible-priced car. That thing is a bit clumsy for shopping trips and sight-seeing.'

'I might know just the thing,' Mack told her. 'Chap who runs the local garage told me the other day that he had a little Peugeot for sale. Geoff Thomas, he's called...Thomas's Garage, just up in the village. He's in the book.'

Patsy thanked him. By the time she had manoeuvred the lorry out of the narrow track she determined to contact Mr Thomas in the morning.

Back home everything was peaceful. Goliath whickered to her as she got out of the lorry, and she gave him and David a slice of carrot and a pat before going into the house, treading rather warily, but the living room was as she had left it. The stove was warm, the cats asleep, and there was no feeling of anything other than quiet comfort. Telling herself that Tabitha's stories were nonsense, Patsy went to bed.

Geoff Thomas's car was just what Patsy needed, small and tidy, with a fair mileage on the clock, but well maintained, and a reasonable price. Pleased, Patsy bought it, and drove it home. Today was a Wednesday, and tomorrow would be the last Thursday in March. Patsy decided that she could do with a trip out, and a proper trial of her new car. She would brave Tabitha's warnings about harrowing sights, and pay a visit to Llanbydder horse sales.

Llanbydder was marked on the map, and Patsy reckoned that the drive would take about an hour. It was a pleasant trip, along quiet roads through rolling countryside. The sun was shining, and Patsy's new car ran smoothly. She was feeling very peaceful by the time she began to see traffic ahead, moving slowly, much of it consisting of cattle lorries and horse trailers, and knew that she was about to arrive.

The road went over a bridge, and Patsy found herself entering a small market town. Cars were parked in every available space, a car park was partly taken over by market stalls, and the rest of it looked to be crowded to overflowing. All the same, Patsy turned into it, and was greeted by a yellow-coated attendant who beckoned to her to follow him. He found her a very narrow space beside a stall selling equestrian supplies of many kinds, and Patsy climbed out into the bright and breezy morning.

There was a steady movement of pedestrians out of the car park and along a narrow street lined with stalls, selling everything from equestrian things to sweets and vegetables. There were also several catering stalls, and a strong smell of frying bacon and onions hung in the air. From ahead Patsy could hear shrill whinnies and the thud of hooves leaving lorries, and soon she found herself at the entrance to the sales yard. A covered entrance yard sheltered the way to the pens, with the sales ring beyond. The narrow gangways between the metal railed pens were wet and slippery from earlier hosing and recent manure, and inside them stood, restlessly, calmly, or frantically, according to temperament, a wide variety of horses and ponies. There were a lot of mountainy ponies, some rough and wild, some sleek and groomed, big cobs, thoroughbreds, little show ponies and one or two huge heavy horses. Some had cards tied to their pens listing their names and breeding, with anxious attendants beside them, others were alone, unshod, some with rough halters hanging from their anxious heads. Those who had hay with them were the envy of those without, who tried to steal a whisp from under the bottom bars of their pens. Some looked well fed and healthy, others were bony and sad, some reached a friendly, curious nose out to an offered hand, and others backed away, one or two snapped, ears flat. Patsy soon knew what Tabitha had meant about harrowing sights. One or two stopped her dead, a physical hurt touching her inside as she looked at a pathetic, ancient little pony with overgrown laminitic feet and hanging head, and further on at a once beautiful Arab stallion, his back now sunken like his eyes, his ribs stark under the greying chestnut coat, but still with an air about him of what he must once have been.

The sale was due to start. People were gathering alongside the long railed run where the horses would be shown, and the auctioneer was on his rostrum at one end, conferring softly with a man in the brown coat of a sales attendant. The first horses to be sold were starting to gather in the space at the end of the run, others queuing in the gangway between the pens. The crowd was cheerful, on a day out, chattering and bright-eyed with the buzz of sales day, and Patsy joined them to watch the first lots sold. A nice looking skewbald, ridden in by the owner, made a good price, a string of ordinary looking ponies went for a few pounds each, and the Arab stallion, Patsy was thankful to see, was quite popular because of his breeding, and went to a competent-looking woman for more than had seemed likely.

There was a second sale ring beyond this one, and Patsy realised from the ponies starting to line up for it that this was the young and unbroken stock. There was a lot of disturbance going on as unhandled ponies were herded towards it along a gangway, and Patsy moved over to watch. The first few were small mountain ponies, yearlings, many of them, wild-eyed and woolly-coated. There were several blank-faced men around the ring, one or two with mobile 'phones clasped to their ears, buying ponies for a couple of pounds each...the meat trade, Patsy realised sadly, as a pretty little dun pony was knocked down to one of them for five pounds. Most of these ponies were the no-hopers, born on the moors, in the sale to make space for sheep, and to bring their farmer owners a few pounds. A few, the especially attractive ones, would find homes as future children's ponies, but too many would not. Patsy was about to turn away, saddened, when the auctioneer's spiel caught her attention, and she turned to see a thin, wild-eyed chestnut cob mare dash down the pen. Her belly was heavy with foal, and her flaxen mane and tail were long and knotted.

'Five-year-old registered cob mare by Bryn Uchaf Highflyer,' said the auctioneer. 'Unbroken, in foal to Cynhaeaf Milgi. A good mare, ladies and gentlemen, fine breeding...Highflyer won the Queen's cup at Builth. What am I bid for this fine mare? One hundred...?'

Patsy stared, riveted. A mare by Emrys's champion cob...but not one that had been well cared for, by the wild and neglected look of her. The auctioneer was rattling on. 'Fifty then...who'll start me at fifty? Thirty...twenty five...? Come on now, think what a foal this mare might give you...'

There was no response. The mare whirled round at the end of the pen and charged back, unshod hooves slipping on the sand spread on the slippery floor of the pen. The attendant at the auctioneer's end turned her with waving arms, and she skidded back, pausing for a moment in front of Patsy with head high, nostrils wide blown, showing the red lining.

'Ten pounds,' Patsy heard herself call. The auctioneer picked it up at once.

'Ten pounds I'm bid...who'll give me twelve? Come on now...'

'Twelve,' said a half-hearted voice from the crowd, and Patsy hesitated. She had given the mare a start...now was the time to stop, and not get carried away. But as the mare set off again, moving with the lovely, high stepping trot of the true Welsh cob, Patsy knew that she was going to bring Emrys's cob's blood back to Bryn Uchaf.

'Fourteen,' she said firmly.

The bidding crept up...reaching fifty pounds as buyers began to eye the mare with more interest.

'I'll lose her,' thought Patsy. 'I can't afford to spend too much.'

But at fifty-five the other bidders were losing heart. The mare slipped again on turning, and trotted lame for a few steps, and suddenly Patsy knew that the cob was hers for the taking.

'Sixty,' she said firmly. There was silence. The auctioneer knew his audience...two minutes later the mare was knocked down to Patsy for sixty pounds.

One of the attendants came to Patsy with his board, and she wrote her name and address and signed it.

'Pay at the office,' the attendant told her. 'Cash only, of course.'

'Oh...' Patsy knew that she had not got sixty pounds on her. She would have to go into the town and find a branch of her bank. Edging out through the crowded gangways she found that her legs were shaking.

'What have I done?' she asked herself, amid the noise of the street market. 'An unbroken mare...and pretty unhandled, by the look of her. For Emrys's sake?'

CHAPTER FOUR

It was too late now for second thoughts. Patsy found the bank, and withdrew the sixty pounds from her not especially healthy account, and made her way back to the sales office. In return for her cash she received the mare's papers, and the certificate of service to the expected foal's sire.

'Bryn Uchaf Eithin Aur,' she read...so that was her new possession's name. She had been number one-hundred-and-ten...Patsy searched until she found the right pen, and stopped to gaze. The mare was standing at the back, as far from the passing people as she could get. Her neck and flanks were patched with sweat, and Patsy could see her trembling. There was no hay in the pen, but a pile was left in the pen next door, from which the occupant had already gone. Patsy picked up a handful, very slowly opened the gate into the pen, and slipped inside. The mare snorted, backing into the corner, and Patsy approached very slowly, holding out the hay. There was a rope halter on the mare's head, so she had at least been touched.

'Come on,' Patsy said softly. She stood still, holding the hay. For a minute the mare remained tensely held away, but hunger won. She reached out her neck and made a desperate grab for the hay. As she munched, Patsy reached out a slow and careful hand, and took hold of the hanging halter rope. The mare shot forward, found her head held, and whirled round Patsy in a circle, almost jerking her off her feet. But then she subsided, snorting, and Patsy was able, for a moment, to touch the tense, sweaty neck. It would do for now...the next problem was how to get her home. For the first time Patsy regretted not having brought the Transit.

Another visit to the office produced a possible transporter, a farmer who was going back towards Pembrokeshire with an empty trailer.

'I'll be turning for Tenby at Cardigan,' he told her. 'But maybe you could pick her up from there...there's a quiet spot behind the cattle market.'

'Yes, I could do that,' agreed Patsy. She hoped that the exchange site really would be quiet. The thought of her new purchase running loose through Cardigan was not a happy one.

A time was fixed, and Patsy, after a final glance at the nervous mare, signed a removal slip for her, and hurried out to collect her car. She would worry about what she had done later, when the mare was home.

Two hours later Patsy was driving into the car park behind the closed cattle market in the Transit. The farmer was already there, parked in a corner. The old horse trailer behind his pick-up van was rocking as the mare inside pawed and kicked.

'You've not picked an easy one there,' he told her, as she lowered the ramp of the lorry. 'Shall I handle her for you?'

'Oh, please,' Patsy was thankful. He was a tough, powerfully built man; the mare would not find it easy to pull away from him and go on the loose.

Eithin Aur came out of the trailer backwards with a rush, her head firmly held by the farmer. She was not happy about entering Patsy's box, but with the halter tight around her nose and Patsy urging from behind she finally charged up the ramp, and was tied up firmly and shortly to one of the strings. Patsy closed the partition, and the farmer threw up the ramp. Inside a volcano erupted as the mare found herself shut in, and Patsy's helper grinned.

'Best get her home as fast as possible,' he said. 'And best of luck with her. That'll be thirty pounds, if you don't mind.'

Patsy paid up, and he drove off, the empty trailer rocking behind him. Patsy was alone with the result of her impulsive purchase.

With the box moving the mare became quiet, obviously concentrating on keeping her balance, but as soon as the lorry stopped in the yard of Bryn Uchaf she let out a piercing whinny and began to kick. There were answering shouts from the field, and David and Goliath appeared at the gate, heads high and ears pricked, their eyes bulging with surprise and excitement. A newcomer, and an exciting one, by the sound of her.

Getting down from the cab Patsy decided that the best place for Eithin Aur would be the smaller field alongside the one in which her old horses were. There was a solid stock fence between the two fields, and the mare would be able to get used to her new friends without any danger of fights, or being chased by them. She was, after all, very much in foal.

The moment the partition went back Eithin Aur made a wild attempt to get free, fighting the rope, and almost hanging herself. There was only one quick way: Patsy always carried a penknife in her pocket, and now she used this to slice through the string to which the rope, for safety, was tied. The mare did not hesitate. Knocking Patsy off her feet, she launched herself from the top of the ramp in an enormous leap, and vanished in the direction of the other horses.

For a moment Patsy could not get up. Her knees and arms hurt, and she felt jarred all over. Slowly, she got hold of the partition and hauled herself to her feet.

'It's your own fault, you stupid old woman,' she told herself. 'Now sort it out.'

Eithin Aur was exchanging squeals and snorts over the gate with David and Goliath. The gate to the smaller field was at right angles to it, and Patsy managed to sidle past the mare and open it. The moment she saw the opening and the green field beyond the mare was gone, her quarters catching Patsy and sending her sideways against the hedge. She went away across the field at a wild, high stepping cob trot, her tail held like a banner, her long mane streaming back from her neck. On the other side of the fence the two old horses charged in pursuit. Weakly Patsy closed the gate and leaned on it, feeling shaken,

Having circled the field a few times the mare paused and turned to consider her neighbours, who were hanging over the stock fence in a fever of curiosity. Snorting, she trotted over to them, showing off, and Patsy knew that once she was fatter, cleaner, and trimmed up she would be quite a spectacular pony.

Reaching out her nose to the others Eithin Aur began to exchange sniffs with them, Goliath with his nose pressed eagerly to hers, David pushing to get his share of the exchange. There was a piercing squeal, and the mare struck out with one fore-foot in the equine equivalent of 'Ooooh...you.' Next moment she was rearing and plunging furiously, one front foot caught in one of the small wire squares which made up the sheep-proof fencing. Alarmed, David and Goliath took off across their field, and Patsy was galvanised into frantic action.

There was a hefty pair of wire cutters in the shed she was using as a store. Patsy ran, age and stiffness forgotten, seized the cutters, and tore back. The mare had stopped fighting. She was standing on three legs, her front foot suspended, still jammed in the wire. Slowly and carefully Patsy approached her, and very slowly, keeping up a murmur of platitudes meant to sooth the mare, she reached out the cutter head, caught the wire between the blades, and pressed the handles together. The wire parted with a sharp snap, the mare shot backwards, and next minute she was standing shaking her head and snorting in the middle of the field. Shaking herself, Patsy subsided onto the grass.

'What stupid, stupid fencing to use with horses,' she said aloud. 'And Emrys was meant to be a horseman...'

Behind her the gate, which she had left open in her haste to reach the mare, slammed shut. Patsy jumped, and started back onto her feet. The wind of course, except that it was blowing quite strongly in the other direction. A brief mini-whirlwind swirled scraps of hay and straw into the air over the yard, and David and Goliath shook their heads and cantered away down the field. Feeling rather unsteady Patsy made her way into the house.

Two cups of tea and half-an-hour later she had recovered. The mare would soon settle, with plenty of time spent taming her, and if she didn't she could always be re-sold. Patsy fetched her handbag from the horse box and settled down to read the mare's registration details with more care.

'Why "Eithin Aur?"' she wondered aloud to the cat, who was sprawled on the mat in front of the stove feeding her kittens. 'I wonder if it's got anything to do with her sire's name, 'Highflyer'? I know it's usual to name foals something that's got a connection with the sire or dam.'

Suddenly the air around her seemed to be charged. The temperature dropped abruptly, the cat leaped up, shedding kittens, and the registration paper was whisked out of Patsy's hand to flutter for a moment before falling to the floor. Patsy started up, half expecting to see Emrys looming over her, but there was nothing there.

'Yes,' said Patsy shakily. 'That's why I bought her...she's your Highflyer's daughter. I thought you'd be pleased to have his blood back here, when he was such a star. And she's in foal...'

For a moment the tension in the air seemed tangible, the cold surrounded Patsy, and she felt the hairs on her arms and the back of her neck starting to rise. Then the shrill ring of the telephone cut through it, and the tension evaporated like a balloon bursting. Feeling breathless, Patsy leaned on a chair for a moment before staggering to answer it.

The caller was Rhiannon.

'John said he was out with the sheep and he heard a lot of whinnying and galloping about over your side,' she said. 'He thought perhaps we should check was there anything wrong?'

'It's very kind of you.' Patsy was touched. 'I'm all right, thanks, I bought a pony today at Llanbydder sale. She's a bit wild.'

'Did you now?' Rhiannon sounded interested. 'What is it...a cob for yourself?'

'She is a cob, but not really for me to ride, not yet, anyway,' Patsy explained. 'She's due to foal quite soon, I should think. She was sired by Emrys's cob, Highflyer...I found a photo of him in the loft. That was why I bought her.'

There was a moment's pause and then, to Patsy's surprise, Rhiannon began to laugh.

'Oh dear,' she said. 'And Emrys so determined not to do just that. Lucky he's not about to see.'

'I don't understand,' Patsy told her. 'Why didn't he want another cob? What happened to Highflyer anyway? Did he die or something?'

'Not with Emrys,' Rhiannon told her. 'It was after he ran into debt with the farm, and had to sell his cob. Never got over it, he didn't, that horse was his pride and joy.'

'So is he still alive?' Patsy asked, thinking how much she would like to see Emrys's stallion.

'No,' Rhiannon sounded quite sad. 'Sold to a top stud, he was, and they fed him up hard to cope with covering all the mares they were sent. Went to his head, did the corn, he was always a very fiery little horse. He got loose and jumped an iron gate to get to some mares, fell and broke a leg. He had to be shot. It made Emrys very bitter, when if it hadn't been for the taxes and restrictions and the falling prices of stock, he would never have sold.'

'But I still don't see why he wouldn't have one of Highflyer's descendants,' said Patsy.

'You didn't know Emrys,' Rhiannon told her. 'Stubborn as an ox, he was. If he couldn't have his Highflyer he wasn't going to settle for what he called second-best, have everyone pitying him for trying to recapture the past.'

'I see...' Patsy began to understand some of the things that had happened. There was one question left to ask.

'What happened to Emrys?' she asked. 'How did he die? I bought this place from the executors, a firm of solicitors. Did he have a heart attack or something? I suppose he was getting on?'

'Fifty-one,' said Rhiannon shortly. 'Lived there all his life, farmed it with his mother after his Da died.' There was a moment's pause, and then she said, 'Well, someone will be telling you if I don't. It was my John who found him...day the bailiffs were due to move him out. Shot himself, he had...out in the yard. John heard it...was why he went over. The gate was blocked by the tractor, and his old dog was dead beside him.'

'Oh...oh God,' Patsy shivered. If she had known, would she ever have bought Bryn Uchaf? The solicitors should have told her, she'd been so carried away by her idea, and the low price of the place, that she had never paused to inquire. No wonder they'd been so quick to accept her offer, and get it all signed and sealed.

'Are you still there?' Rhiannon sounded concerned. 'I'm sorry, I should have told you sooner. Are you all right?'

'Yes...' Patsy knew that she sounded shocked. 'I'm all right. I...I should have guessed there was something like that.'

It was amazing that Tabitha had not told her...although she had dropped hints about a strangeness to do with Emrys. No doubt Mack had told her to keep quiet.

'Would you like me to come over?' Rhiannon obviously felt guilty for telling the story.

'No...no, it's all right, I'm fine...just sorry. I can imagine how Emrys must have felt,' Patsy told her.

When Rhiannon had hung up Patsy went slowly back into the living room. The cat was back with her kittens, and the registration document was lying where it had fallen. Taking a deep breath, Patsy picked it up, and then faced the empty room.

'I'm sorry,' she said. 'I'm sorry for what happened to you, and to Highflyer, and I'm sorry I bought Eithin Aur without knowing. But she's here now, and so am I, this is my home, and I...I want to stay. Please try to accept that.'

There was no reaction, and Patsy suddenly felt foolish, standing talking to an empty room. She was beginning to feel her bruises now, and reaction was setting in. She was tired, suspecting that she had made an unwise purchase, and on top of that was Rhiannon's depressing news about Emrys. Patsy decided to make herself a cup of tea, get the old horses settled early, and have something hot and soothing for supper before having an early night.

In spite of following these plans Patsy slept badly. She was sore from the fall that Eithin Aur had given her, and disturbed by the mare's calls for company in the night, and Goliath's answering roars. By morning she was so stiff that it was hard to get dressed.

'You can say "I told you so,"' she informed Emrys, if he was listening. 'Maybe it'll make you happier.'

She fed the cat, and the old horses, and made up a tempting bowl of sliced carrots and green Alfa-A chaff to offer the mare, who was standing in the middle of the field staring at her with head and tail high. When Patsy opened the gate she turned and made off to the far end of the field at her showy trot.

'I'm not chasing you,' Patsy told her. 'If you want breakfast you'll have to come and get it.'

She placed a sheaf of hay beside the bowl and went to lean on the gate and wait. From her place by the far bank Eithin Aur watched her suspiciously. Patsy gazed around at the morning. It was spring today, the light brilliant, so clear that it hurt the eyes, and there was a wonderful smell of growing things and sweet earth. The banks were thick with primroses, their scent warm and wild on the breeze.

As Patsy remained by the gate without moving, unthreatening, the mare relaxed a little, and began to edge closer, breaking into a trot, and circling the food. Two rabbits emerged from the hedge and began to nibble grass, and Patsy saw the tawny flash of a fox slip over the bank. Overhead two buzzards circled slowly, rising steadily higher on a warm up-draught, and Eithin Aur decided that it was safe to grab a mouthful of the hay. The feed bowl was a strange object. Chewing the hay she backed off a step, staring at it, then lowered her head to sniff. The contents smelled good. Very gingerly she stretched her neck, still sniffing, and then, very daring, she grabbed a mouthful of the feed and immediately shot backwards, chewing and tossing her head.

'Good, isn't it? Patsy asked her, from the gate. The mare stared at her, and then raised her nose high, rolling back her lips and turning the top one up from her teeth, testing this new taste on the back of her tongue with glands that checked both taste and smell together. It obviously pleased her, for she came back more boldly for a second mouthful, and soon she was eating eagerly, although she raised her head to prick her ears warily towards Patsy between each fresh mouthful.

Patsy waited at the gate until the mare had finished, and then she turned back towards the house. There was a stir, a shifting of the light, and for a moment Patsy thought that she saw a figure there behind her, also watching the mare, but it was gone as she tried to focus on it.

'Nice, isn't she?' she said aloud. 'A credit to Highflyer, do you think?'

There was no reply, but a sudden puff of wind sent some whisps of hay flying from the barn where it was stored, and Patsy saw the cat, who had been hunting mice in there, shoot out of the door with her tail brushed up.

'Oh, for goodness sake...' Patsy decided to face it out, if that was possible with a ghost. She turned towards the barn, but as she reached the door she hesitated. It was dark in there, beside the pile of bales...dark, and somehow uninviting. Next minute there was a swishing sound, and suddenly the pile of bales was tipping towards her. Turning to run Patsy stumbled, and one of the falling bales hit her on the shoulder, sending her sprawling. Seeing the others tipping Patsy rolled sideways frantically, as the rest of the bales thudded down in the place where she had been standing. Loose hay whirled across the yard, and Patsy scrambled to her feet, shaking. She was covered in mud, her shoulder aching and her hands grazed. There was hay all over the yard.

'What...what was that for?' she asked shakily. 'I didn't mean to taunt you...'

Nothing happened. The sun shone, the shadows seemed to disperse, and the cat came to rub around Patsy's ankles as she brushed hay and mud from her clothes. For the first time, though, Patsy felt that she was under threat.

'I can't leave,' she thought, making her way shakily towards the house. 'What would I do? This is my place now...somewhere for me and the horses...somehow I've just got to get Emrys to accept that...and me.'

She was finishing breakfast when she heard the sudden clatter of hooves in the yard, and going out she found Mack sitting on Osbourne, lighting a cigarette, while David and Goliath stared at him over their gate. Osbourne was pulling hay from one of the fallen bales, and as Patsy appeared Mack dismounted.

'It looks as if you could do with a hand,' he said. 'Going into the barn, are they?'

'Er...yes,' Patsy was grateful. 'Thank you.'

He gave her Osbourne's reins to hold, and while Patsy was still wondering whether stacking the bales back might be too much for him at his age he began to re-stack them as easily as Gareth had.

'Done,' he said, five minutes later. 'I say...not hurt are you?' He had noticed her grazed hands and the mud still down one side of her jeans.

'No...I'm fine...just a bit of trouble with my new purchase...out there.' Patsy gestured towards the field where the cob had begun to graze again, well away from the gate.

'I say...' Mack went for a closer look. 'Where did you get that one?'

'I went to have a look at Llanybidder, and to try out my new car,' explained Patsy. 'And I came home with her. She's by Highflyer...Emrys's old cob.'

'Ah,' Mack sounded as if he understood. 'Looks as if you'll soon have two of them.'

'Yes...she's in foal to another cob,' Patsy told him. 'She looked as if she could do with a bit of care and good food, so I thought perhaps I owed it to her in a way, as I've bought Emrys's old place.'

'I wonder what the old boy would have thought of that,' said Mack. 'Maybe he would have approved, when he saw her. Bit funny about losing his old stallion, by all accounts.'

'Yes, I've heard that,' agreed Patsy. She could not help glancing towards the barn, but there was no sign of movement, and the shadows looked benign. The cat was sitting in the doorway with her paws tucked under her, and some sparrows were pecking about above her on the recently disturbed bales.

'Good luck with her, anyway,' Mack turned back from the gate and took Osbourne's reins from Patsy. 'I called round to see if you felt like a ride along the tops, as it's a nice day.'

'I'd love to come, but maybe not today.' Patsy was aware of feeling sore in many places after the traumas of the last two days. 'I'll leave Goliath to get used to his new friend today, I think'

Mack agreed cheerfully, and Osbourne clattered off down the lane. Patsy went into the house in search of coffee.

After that first reaction Emrys...or what Patsy had come to think of as Emrys...remained quiet. Eithin Aur settled in her field, and Patsy spent hours sitting in the grass beside bowls of feed until the mare would come and eat with her there, The next step was to persuade Eithin Aur to let herself be touched, and then to accept the head collar which Patsy very slowly and gently slipped over her nose and buckled behind her ears. Once that was done it was much simpler to get the mare to allow herself to be caught and held on a rope while she ate, and Patsy felt that she was really accomplishing something.

It was full spring now, the season sweeping a wash of brilliant green and shining spring colours over the countryside. Every bank was a mass of primroses, gorse flamed in banks of brilliant gold, and in gardens everywhere blossom was coming out, pink and white and foaming. This was this country's show time, when flowers that no longer grew wild anywhere else in Britain took over in a breathtaking display that seemed to belong to a younger time when the air was clearer and the world less crowded. There were swallows now, flashing through the bright air, and rebuilding the old nests that were in every barn and stable

One brilliant day, when the light was almost too bright for comfort, Patsy took her promised ride over the top with Mack. Goliath laboured gamely in Osbourne's wake, scrambling up the steep path which led between rocky crags to the ancient golden road, the old pack and pilgrim trail along the top of the Preseli range. They paused at the top to look round. In the distance on three sides the sea sparkled brilliant blue to the horizon, while beyond the edge of the moor lay the small patchwork fields of Pembrokeshire, the sparkling white cottages, and small green woods. The air smelled sweetly of flowers and upland grass, and the light breeze lifted the horses' manes. Overhead circled two of the inevitable buzzards, and small brown birds fluttered, chirruping, among the rocks. Then Mack turned Osbourne, and set the big horse into a gallop, and Goliath, thrilled, thundered in pursuit. Skylarks rose in front of them, the warm breeze blew into Patsy's face, and she felt young again, young and free and exhilarated. Life was good, and as they returned home along the quiet lanes she invited Mack to bring Tabitha over for a meal later in the week.

***

It was a long time since Patsy had done any social catering. She decided to keep it simple, melon to start with, then a good casserole, cooked long and slowly in the Rayburn, followed by an apple crumble. They were due at seven thirty. Patsy had the house tidy, flowers on the dresser, and the table set. There were also flowers in the front room, where she had her comfortable chairs and settee, and her own heavy velvet curtains in place of Emrys's old cotton ones. Feeling something in the air, she kept a tight eye on the Rayburn: she was not going to risk any of Emrys's tricks tonight. Right on time she heard Mack's car drive into the yard, and she went to open the front door to them. The big knob turned, but it would not open. Annoyed, Patsy tugged, but the door remained tightly shut.

'All right,' Patsy told the empty hallway. 'I'll let them in at the back.'

The back door refused to open as well. Furious, Patsy tugged at it, and then turned to face the room.

'Stop it,' she said. 'This isn't fair. It's my home now, I can invite anyone I like...'

She heard the front door knocker drop, and suddenly she felt close to tears. It was all so stupid, and so impossible.

'Please,' she said shakily. 'Please Emrys...let them in.'

Without much hope, she went to the front door, but this time, to her relief, it opened. Mack and Tabitha stood outside, Mack looking rather surprised, Tabitha with a secret smile on her face.

'I'm sorry to be so long, the door stuck,' Patsy told them, knowing that she sounded flustered. 'Come in...'

They came, Tabitha looking round, still with that smile.

'Well', she said. 'It is looking nice. The old boy would hardly know it, if he was around.'

'Which I'm sure he isn't, ' said Mack, rather pointedly.

Patsy settled them in the front room, poured drinks, and checked the meal. All seemed in order.

Before going back to her guests she paused.

'Thank you,' she whispered. 'I appreciate it.'

The rest of the evening went smoothly, and Patsy felt her confidence returning. The doors had stuck, that was all; she must stop imagining Emrys whenever anything did not go to plan. All the same, she could not help giving a sigh of relief when Mack and Tabitha left. Whatever the truth, having guests had proved rather a strain.

***

Eithin Aur's belly dropped, and she began to move a little less lightly. The foal must be due in the next month, Patsy thought, watching her as sparkling April turned to softer May. Meeting Rhiannon at the local post office one day, Patsy asked her what the mare's name meant in English.

'Eithin Aur,' repeated Rhiannon. 'Golden Gorse...now there's a pretty name for your pony.'

It was, although it had nothing to do with her sire's name. Perhaps she could change that when she named the foal, thought Patsy.

David and Goliath were turned out at night now, and the kittens were weaned and haunted the stables and barns, hunting with their mother. Lying in bed with the window partly open Patsy could hear the living night outside, the horses cropping grass and snorting, and sometimes, as the first touch of dawn lightened the sky, galloping in wild delight at the freedom and the freshness and the new young grass. Owls called from the wood, foxes barked in the fields and the banks, and the kittens brought their catches to their mother for inspection, calling in loud, demanding 'prrps' for her attention.

Although nothing spectacular had happened Patsy had to accept that she was not alone in the house. She rarely saw or heard 'Emrys' but there was a sense of him in the rooms, and especially in the yard and the fields. Living alone in such a place Patsy knew was making her both more fanciful and more perceptive, and it was a stronger sense than usual of this presence that woke her suddenly one morning at first light.

'What?' she asked the empty room, sitting up in bed, and then she heard Goliath whinny outside, and a low, deep whicker that she had never heard before...a sound of maternal pride and comfort. Patsy scrambled out of bed and went to the window. She could only see part of her fields because of the ash trees which sheltered the house, but she could see Goliath's white rump through the branches as he stood close to the dividing fence. Throwing on some clothes, Patsy ran downstairs and out into the fresh early morning, subconsciously registering the sense of company which went with her.

The mare had foaled at the far end of the field, in a sheltering corner of the banks, and as Patsy went carefully down the field towards her, with David and Goliath trotting interestedly along on the other side of the fence, the foal staggered to its feet. Thrilled, Patsy stopped to stare. It was a chestnut like its mother, short-bodied and long-legged with a tiny seahorse head and a coat still damp and crumpled from the womb. The mare raised her head from licking her baby to stare anxiously at Patsy and the foal butted her side, searching for milk.

'You clever girl,' said Patsy softly. 'Isn't she clever, Emrys? A grand-baby for your Highflyer...surely that's a good sight?'

The foal found the teat and began to suck, raising its tiny brush of a tail, blond, like its mother's. Peering Patsy saw that it was a colt. Eithiun Aur turned her head to nuzzle him, pushing him gently closer to her, and Patsy said softly, 'Well, how about it? Could he be a new entry for the Royal Welsh one day, under the Bryn Uchaf name?'

There was no response, but no tension either. Watching the foal feed, Patsy felt a warm rush of euphoria. It was wonderful, this new life on this soft, bright morning, and she wanted someone with whom to share it. She could tell Rhiannon or Mack, or 'phone Katy, but suddenly and foolishly Patsy found herself wishing that Emrys, the one person who might really share this moment, was something more than a shadow.

'Fool,' she told herself, feeling her eyes smart with sudden tears...of what? Joy...regret for what could not be...a sense of the beauty and miracle of life, and sorrow for its shortness? Sitting down on the grass she settled to watch for a while as Eithin Aur's baby enjoyed his first meal.

A little later Patsy did 'phone Katy, and her daughter sounded almost as thrilled as she had been.

'A foal!' she exclaimed. 'Oh Mum, I'd love to see him...we never had a mare foal in all the time I had horses.'

'You could always come down,' Patsy told her, and for a moment Katy hesitated. Then she said, 'I would...but Andrew...if I go off...'

She stopped, but Patsy understood, and sadly registered the insecurity, and the obsession behind it. Why had bright, lively, 'up for it' Katy chosen Andrew, handsome, charming, and fickle, with his wife always hovering in the wings, in two minds about whether to demand him back.

'Take photographs,' Katy asked now. 'Lots of them...and when I can I'll come. I could have a ride on old Golly too...it's ages since I had a ride.'

There was a note of loss in her voice, and Patsy saw again the eager, competitive, horse-mad young girl with her dedication and drive, with whom she had shared so many tense, exciting, and sometimes triumphant horsey moments. There were times when the loss of that girl cut her with deep regret for times passed.

'It would be really good to see you,' she told Katy now.

'I'll try,' Katy promised. 'I really will.'

They hung up, and Patsy turned rather sadly away from the telephone. Was there any hope, she wondered, of Katy ever finding secure happiness with Andrew?

CHAPTER FIVE

During the next few weeks the foal gained strength rapidly, trotting and cantering round his mother, butting her with his hard little head when he wanted food, and experimenting with kicks and bucks. When Patsy fed the mare he came with her, intensely curious, wanting his nose in the bowl as well. Patsy was giving the mare extra feed now, and the foal mouthed it, lifting his lip to taste. If Patsy kept still he would come up to her, sniffing her clothes and hair and nibbling with tiny milk teeth. Patsy became able to stroke him on his woolly neck, so long as Eithin Aur was occupied with food, but any attempt to handle him more seriously, such as putting a foal slip onto his head, brought her hurriedly placing herself between them. Patsy worried that, according to all the advice she read, a foal should be haltered and taught to lead as early as possible, but so far it was not proving possible, in spite of all the hours she spent with them in the field.

Sometimes, at dusk, the foal and his mother would run, the mare fast, the foal galloping ahead on his long legs, as light as air with his tiny body, setting off the two old horses in the next field so that the air shook with the thunder of hooves.

'What shall we call him?' Patsy asked the invisible spectator that she knew was nearby, also watching the flying foal as dusk thickened the light and the bats began to swoop after midges.

There was no reply, but some words formed slowly in Patsy's mind.

'Aur...Hedfa Aur...Golden...Golden Flight.'

'Golden Flight.' Patsy spoke the name aloud. 'Why not? Thanks Emrys.'

With all the attention it gradually became easier for Patsy to handle the mare. Eithin Aur accepted being led now, and she would come into the stable, her foal trotting behind, for Patsy to brush her and look at her feet. There were swallows about the yard now, swooping and diving for insects, and taking possession of their old nests in the barn and stable, and as May gave way to June, the spring flowers were replaced by the summer blooming, tall spikes of purple foxgloves, wild roses, honeysuckle, and in sheltered places shy, sweet small orchids. Mack organised a barbecue in his garden, to which he and Tabitha invited most of the district, and Patsy lived with open windows, glad of the house's thick, cool stone walls as the weather became hot.

The best times for riding now were early morning or in the evening, and Patsy and Goliath, sometimes with David trotting alongside, sometimes with Mack, but most often on their own, explored the moors and the hills, and the deep, peaceful lanes. Eithin Aur and her baby spent most of the hot daylight hours standing deep in the shelter of an overhanging hawthorn hedge, against a bank riddled with rabbit holes.

The foal was endlessly curious. To keep him away from the treacherous stock fencing Patsy invested in an electric fence set, power pack, tapes, and plastic poles, and a battery to power it. After one sniff, and a prick on his sensitive nose, the foal kept well away. Patsy thought that she had made the field as safe as possible, but one early morning she woke to hear Eithin Aur whinnying loudly, not at all with her usual maternal call, and going to the window she could see glimpses of the mare through the ash branches, trotting along beside the bank where she and the foal usually sheltered. The foal was not in sight.

Throwing on some clothes Patsy ran downstairs, stampeding the indignant cat, who had been hoping for an early breakfast. Hurrying across the field with David and Goliath trotting along on the other side of the fence, she could see the mare standing staring at the thick hedge on the bank, and she could also see a gleam of chestnut hair in the hedge, but much higher up than it had any right to be. Pushing her way under the overhanging thorn branches Patsy saw that the foal had been exploring, scrambling up the stony bank until he was balanced precariously on the top between two stout hawthorn trunks. He was stuck, his legs entangled in old spiky branches, and his small body jammed between the bushes. As Patsy appeared below him, and his mother began to call again, he began to struggle, squirming and plunging, and getting even more jammed. Patsy knew that there was no time to 'phone for help if she was to rescue him before he was seriously injured. She scrambled up the bank, hardly noticing the sharp thorns catching her hands and clothes, and reached out until she could touch the foal's nose. His only hope was to go backwards, and at the pressure on his nose he did just that, flinging himself back and suddenly breaking free. Below, Eithin Aur whinnied again, and the foal launched himself off the bank to get to her, landing on nose and knees in the field below.

Letting go of the spiky branch onto which she was holding Patsy slithered after him. The foal was pressed close to his mother, trembling, and to Patsy's alarm there was bright blood pouring from a gash in his chest. She had to get him into the stable, and call the vet.

Eithin Aur had relaxed now that her baby was back beside her. She seemed unconscious of his injuries now that he was pressed to her side, and when Patsy brought some pony nuts in a bowl she plunged her nose in, and let Patsy clip on the rope and start to lead her in. At the gate, however, she jibbed. She had been led about in the field, but Patsy had not brought her into the yard since her arrival. Taking a firmer hold of the rope, Patsy held the feed bowl a tempting few inches in front of the mare, but she had become nervous, and Patsy knew from her tense stance that at any moment Eithin Aur would dive backwards and she would lose her hold of the rope. They had to come in...the foal had to have treatment.

'Come on girl, come on...please...' Patsy shook the feed in the bowl, but the mare was no longer interested. The foal pressed close, still shaking, and the mare was starting to sense that something was wrong, but she was connecting it with the yard.

'It isn't going to work,' Patsy thought, with a flash of panic, and at the same moment Eithin Aur leaped forward as if she had been slapped, and a moment later the door to the big old pen, once a bull pen, swung open. Patsy knew, with startled relief, that she had help.

Eithin Aur was on her way across the yard now, glancing back over her shoulder. Startled, she almost dragged Patsy into the pen, and the foal came in beside her. Behind them the door slammed, and the mare whirled round, head high, staring.

'Thanks Emrys,' Patsy said, almost before she could think. It was nonsense, of course, it had to be, and yet...but it was not time to worry about Emrys at the moment. The blood was still running fast down the foal's front leg from the jagged hole in his chest, and Patsy knew that she had to try to control it before she went in to 'phone the vet. She needed a pad...something clean to apply pressure...guiltily she knew that there was nothing suitable in her first aid kit...in fact it hardly existed. She had a clean tee shirt on...only a bra under it, but there was no-one to see...she pulled it off, folding it into a pad, and pressed it firmly against the wound. The foal jumped, cowering against his mother, but the blood was still flowing, rapidly soaking through the white shirt, and Patsy knew that she needed something more. The colt was so little...how long would it take him to bleed to death? The blood was not pumping, as from an artery, but the flow was free and fast.

There was a sudden draught, a rising breeze, and a coldness in the air. In the corner of the pen a thickly clustered mass of cobwebs lifted and stirred, although nothing else moved: the straw on the floor remained still, so did Eithin Aur's tail. Cobwebs...in the back of Patsy's mind memory stirred of an old story read...a historical romance, in which the local witch had saved the hero's life by packing his wound with cobwebs. That was fitting enough, as she must look at the moment, with her greying hair falling into her eyes and her scraggy breasts as good as bare, taking advice, it seemed, from a ghost, for what else would draw her attention to the cobwebs in such a way?

Patsy relaxed the pressure from her pad, and seized a handful of the sticky webs. They did not look hygienic but the vet would surely sort out any possible infection when she was able to get to the telephone to call him. The wound was not wide, but deep: a stake from the hedge had caused it, and a rolled handful of the webs packed the hole. Patsy followed it with a second, and then re-applied pressure from the blood soaked pad. It was working. The flowing blood had slowed to a trickle, and when she carefully took the pad away there was no more than a light seepage. Patsy felt a warm breath on her neck as the mare turned to see what was happening, and seemed satisfied that there was no danger from Patsy to her baby. Weakly, Patsy got up from her knees, and let herself out of the pen to head for the telephone.

***

The vet's telephone number, given to her by Rhiannon, was beside the 'phone, and the receptionist who answered promised to contact him on his mobile and get him to Patsy as soon as possible. Patsy's instinct was to get straight back to the foal, but reason told her to get cleaned up first, and to find another shirt.

By the time she returned to the foal he was rather half-heartedly feeding, but he did not look in immediate danger of collapse.

Patsy was filling a bucket with fresh water for the mare when the vet's mud-splattered Land Rover clattered over the cattle grid into the yard.

The vet was a tall, youngish man, mainly bald, wearing jeans and a plaid shirt.

'Simon Mason,' he introduced himself, and Patsy could hear that he was English. 'Now, what's this foal been up to?'

The foal had lain down, and Eithin Aur was eating hay. She did not object when the vet knelt down beside her baby. The foal, not so confident, scrambled rather shakily to his feet, and Simon said, 'That's a good sign, he isn't too weak. Ah, someone knows the old remedies. Spider web's antifungal and antibacterial, rich in vitamin K, good at making blood clot; a remedy worthy of old Emrys himself.'

'So they won't have done any harm?' Patsy asked him, and the vet said that he doubted it.

'It isn't too bad,' he said. 'It would have been dangerous if the bleeding hadn't stopped, but you did the right thing in using desperate measures to stop it. A little fellow like this one hasn't too much blood to lose. I'll clean him up, and pop in a couple of stitches, and he should be fine. It's amazing what trouble these little ones get into, and recover from. Nice little fellow...How is he bred?'

Patsy told him, and the vet looked at her and raised his eyebrows.

'Emrys's old cob, eh?' he said. 'Now, that should please the old boy...if he's still around to know.'

'I sometimes think he is,' Patsy told him, and the vet grinned.

'Yes...cobwebs,' he said thoughtfully. 'Why not? He was a horseman of the old school, was Emrys...'

He turned away to fetch his bag from the Land Rover, while Patsy watched him thoughtfully, gently rubbing the foal behind his ears so that he relaxed, turning sleepy now after the shock. No-one, she thought, seemed to find the idea of Emrys's continuing influence particularly impossible. Was there something about this country, with its other-worldliness, and feeling of magic, that made the impossible seem, if not likely, at least imaginable?

The vet put in two stitches, re-packed his bag, and departed, telling Patsy to keep mother and son in until next day, and to telephone if she was worried. Feeling very sore and shaky, now that the crisis was over, Patsy went indoors to deal with her own scratches and shock.

There was a bottle on the kitchen table, and a glass. Patsy stopped short. She was sure that she had not put them there, and the vet had not been near the house. She did not even remember seeing the bottle before: it was whisky, one that she recognised from the label as a good old malt, something that she would never have bought herself. The bottle was half-full.

'I don't drink whisky,' said Patsy aloud. 'Nasty stuff.'

Something gave her a firm shove in the back, and she found herself in a chair at the table.

'Ohh...all right,' Patsy was half amused and half alarmed. Was she really in shock, or was this really happening?

'No use arguing with a ghost,' she decided, and she poured a small measure of the smooth golden liquid. Sipping it made her shudder, but there was no doubt that after a few minutes she did feel less shaky, and more prepared to finding antiseptic and plasters for the cuts and scratches that the thorns had made on her hands and arms.

'All right Emrys,' she said aloud. 'You were right...I'm beginning to wonder how I'd manage without you.'

There was a kind of shiver in the air, and the back door, which Patsy had left open, swung suddenly shut

'I've embarrassed him,' thought Patsy wonderingly. Either she was going completely crazy or she was dealing with a ghost with current emotions.

'Crazy, that must be it,' decided Patsy. 'Senile, I suppose. It comes of living alone, or that's what Katy would tell me. She said this would happen. But so what? It really doesn't bother me at all.'

The foal made good, rapid progress. When the vet came again a few days later the stitches had already dissolved and the cut was healthily scabbed.

'Will it leave a scar?' Patsy asked, thinking of her idea for showing the foal, and the vet shrugged.

'It is possible,' he said. 'Try applying some Cornucrescine when the scab has gone...unless Emrys has a better idea.'

He drove off laughing, and Patsy tried to smile herself. No doubt the whole district would soon dub her crazy, but as she had decided before, so what?

It was another beautiful day. High summer lay over the hills and fields, dog roses, honeysuckle, and foxgloves tangled in the hedgerows and grew along the banks, and out on the moor the buzzards drifted on the warm, rising air and the furze smelled of vanilla. Patsy saddled Goliath and together they climbed, slowly, for it was very warm, to the top of the great green hills, until they were high enough to become a part of the timeless landscape. They were in the midst of a great silence, not broken today by any sound of civilization; not even the jets were active. Patsy remembered tales told of these ancient hills, of fairies and monsters, of the Iron Age settlements, and the grave of King Arthur. There was the story of the strange mist, which could suddenly appear, blanking out the view, until it shifted to give the traveller a glimpse of the world of fairy.

The air, and the stillness and the sense of endless time, soothed the soul, and both Patsy and Goliath were in a mood of sleepy content as they made their way home through the fords and along the deep, scented lanes. The farm waited, bathed in afternoon sunlight, shadows spreading towards the buildings. A mirror of insects danced above the sheltered yard, and dragonflies swooped and darted above the stream which ran across the corner and under a plank bridge where a footpath led away into the wood.

Dismounting, Patsy became aware of a disturbance in the peace. There was something charged, a vibration in the air which she could not fathom. Eithin Aur and her foal were grazing contentedly in their field, and David was looking over his stable door. The cat slept in a patch of shade on the garden bank, and two of her kittens were crouched one on either side of a hopeful hole below her.

'Emrys?' said Patsy doubtfully, feeling a fool, but nothing happened. She led Goliath into his stable and knew at once that he sensed something as well. Instead of going straight to his water bucket, or rubbing his sweaty head against the wall, he crowded close behind her as she let herself out of his stable, pushing to get his head over the door. Patsy bolted it behind her and heard a faint sound from David's box...a sound that did not belong, a muffled human sob. There was someone in David's stable with him.

'Who's there?' Patsy peered past the brown pony into the shadowy depths of his stable. There was someone there, someone huddled at the back, sitting with their back to the rear wall and their arms wrapped around their knees. Then David moved, turning towards the figure, and as it raised its head the light caught it and Patsy recognised her daughter.

'Katy,' she exclaimed. 'What is it? What's happened?'

'Mum...' Katy stumbled to her feet, pushed past the pony, shoved the door open, and flung herself into her mother's arms. 'He...he's left me...he and Amanda...they...they've emigrated to New Zealand...he'd been planning it...never told me...'

She was sobbing and hot and damp. Patsy hugged her awkwardly; hugging and cuddling had never come easily to her, and after a moment Katy pulled away, raising a hand to push her thick, fair hair away from her face. She was a tall girl, taller than Patsy, but thin and finely built, with sharp cheek bones and wide apart blue eyes. At the moment her face was flushed and puffy, and her hair looked lank and greasy. Her clothes, jeans and a blue tee shirt, were crumpled.

'Let's go inside,' Patsy told her. 'You look as if you could do with something to drink and eat. Where are your things? And haven't you come by car?'

'It...it was in the garage, being serviced, I had to get the train,' Katy rubbed her eyes, more like a child than a woman of twenty-six. 'I didn't bring much...I just wanted to get away...he left me a note...And then I 'phoned from the station at Carmarthen, and you didn't answer...I had to get a taxi...'

She gave another sob, and Patsy decided to be brisk.

'Come on', she said. 'Let's get inside, and put the kettle on, and you can tell me the whole story. It sounds typical Andrew to me.'

'You would say that.' Katy was immediately angry. 'You never liked him.'

'No, I didn't,' agreed Patsy. 'And it seems I was right.'

'Why did I come?' Katy hung back. 'I might have known I wouldn't get any sympathy.'

'I am sympathetic,' Patsy told her. 'I wish for your sake that Andrew had proved me wrong, and made you happy.'

She took the back door key from under the brick where she had left it and led the way inside. Following, Katy stopped dead, surprised out of her pre-occupation with Andrew.

'Why,' she said. 'It...it's different...nice...'

'What did you expect?' Patsy was amused. Katy shook her head and went slowly to sit down by the table, still looking around.

'I don't really know,' she said. 'I suppose...something smaller...and shabbier...not a real old farmhouse like this...and all the lovely wood...'

'You can't think much of my sense,' said Patsy drily. 'Did you think I'd buried myself in some sort of slum?'

'I...well...yes, I did, in a way,' admitted Katy. 'It all seemed so odd...and I always thought of Wales as a bit sort of slummy...rural slums, all Welshmen shagging sheep and singing in chapel...and the valleys...'

There was a stir in the air and the door to the front room slammed shut. Katy jumped, and Patsy tried not to smile. Emrys was offended.

'What was that?' asked Katy. 'It isn't windy...is there someone else here?'

'A secret man friend, you mean? asked Patsy. 'One of your sheep-shagging, chapel-going Welshmen? What if there is?'

'Mum,' Katy sounded alarmed. 'You...you haven't...?'

'Oh no, of course not...anyway, chance would be a fine thing.' Patsy grinned. That would probably annoy Emrys even more. 'It must have been a draught...now, something to eat. Bacon and eggs?'

'I don't know if I can eat,' Katy was reminded of her troubles, 'A cup of coffee though...I've been travelling for hours...'

'Well, I'm hungry anyway,' Patsy told her. 'I'll make us a nice, unhealthy fry-up.'

She loaded the frying pan well with bacon, knowing Katy's tastes and appetite, and soon the mouth-watering smell filled the air and brought the cats eagerly in from the garden. Leaning down from her chair, Katy picked up the pretty little tortoiseshell kitten and the mother cat went over to sniff and inspect her.

'They're sweet.' Katy tickled the kitten's chin and the air vibrated with its purr. 'And I haven't seen the foal yet...you know Mum, you look really well. I never thought you'd really do this.'

'Move down here?' Patsy tipped the bacon onto a warm plate, broke eggs into the pan, and put the bacon to keep warm in the bottom oven of the Rayburn. 'I wanted out of that house in Surrey after your father died. I'd hated it there for years; it felt like a trap. And apart from you as a child it didn't hold happy memories, with your father's illness and everything that meant.'

'I can understand that,' agreed Katy. 'But to come so far...I know we had some holidays down here when I was little, although I don't remember much about the countryside, but I'd have thought somewhere closer to...well, life.'

'There's plenty of life down here,' Patsy told her. 'It just isn't lived at the same pace.'

The eggs cooked, and some tomatoes to go with them, and they sat down to eat. Katy seemed to have forgotten that she wasn't hungry. She was soon eating the fry-up as eagerly as the cats, who were squabbling over bits of bacon rind on the kitchen floor. Patsy cut thick slices of fruit cake to follow, and then made more coffee.

'Now,' she said, when they were drinking it. 'Do you want to talk, or shall we go outside and look at the foal, and turn out the old boys?'

'Let's go outside.' Katy stood up restlessly. 'I've been sitting in trains and taxis all day.'

Eithin Aur and her foal came up at a trot to see what treats were on offer, and Katy went into ecstasies about the foal.

'He's gorgeous,' she exclaimed. 'Oh, I would love to have seen him when he was brand new. And what a pretty mare.'

Eithin Aur accepted Katy's hand on her neck a little nervously, as she was still doubtful of strangers. The foal came boldly to nibble and sniff, and Patsy left Katy to play with them while she sprayed David and Goliath with anti-midge spray and led them out to their field. The sun was low now, sinking towards the sea, and the high, wide sky was barred with strips of purple cloud. The horses moved away to graze, and Katy leaned on the gate, watching them, and the changing colours in the sky.

'It is beautiful,' she said. 'So wide and bright and clear, you never get light or skies like this in Surrey. Too much pollution. I...I suppose you do in New Zealand.'

'I doubt if that's why Andrew has gone there,' said Patsy briskly. 'He always was one to take an easy way out, and what could be an easier way than this? Out of reach, and his marriage saved, in one big step. I remember him talking about the opportunities in New Zealand when I knew him.'

'I know.' Katy was starting to cry again, the distraction of the horses and the country fading. 'He talked about it to me as well. I...I thought he might suggest we went together...leaving Amanda behind. I would have gone, too, he knew that...I'd have gone anywhere.'

'Yes, I know,' said Patsy, but she refused to encourage Katy's despair. 'I never could understand why. Look love, face it, it never was any good long-term, was it? The times he's made you frantic and miserable, breaking promises, drifting back to Amanda...this really had to come.'

'You're glad.' Katy was getting hysterical again. 'You wanted this to happen...you don't care how I feel so long as you're proved right. I should never have come here, expecting sympathy, I'm going...I'm going now...'

'Katy...' began Patsy, but Katy had flounced off across the yard. Patsy had left the back door open, but now it suddenly slammed in Katy's face. Katy stopped dead, and Patsy sighed. Emrys obviously disapproved of hysterical females. By the time she reached the door Katy was trying to open it, tugging angrily at the handle.

'This stupid door,' she shouted. 'I knew this place would be a wreck. First it slams shut, now it's jammed.'

'Let me,' said Patsy, but the handle still refused to turn.

'It's just stiff.' Patsy was not going to mention Emrys to Katy, who would then be quite convinced that her mother was crazy. 'There's a can of WD 40 in the shed, will you get it?'

Katy flounced off and Patsy looked at the glass panel in the door.

'Come on Emrys,' she said. 'She's upset, give her a break, and let us in.'

For a moment the door remained shut, then the handle turned and it swung open, just as Katy returned with the spray can.

'It's all right, I've done it,' Patsy told her. 'Now come in and calm down. You can't start back tonight anyway, there won't be a train for hours. Let's sort out somewhere for you to sleep, and if you want to, you can go back to London in the morning.'

'Oh, all right.' Katy gave in. 'But just stop sniping about Andrew. Even if you're right I don't want to hear it.'

The spare room had a bed in it, an old single bed that had once been Katy's, but it was surrounded by the debris that Patsy had dumped in there when she first arrived, boxes of paperback books, a crate of spare china, a pile of spare bedding, and some spare furniture, an old chair, two damaged coffee tables, and an old standard lamp.

'It looks like a jumble sale,' said Katy, and Patsy had to agree.

'I've been meaning to sort it out', she said. 'But there's been so much else to do and think about. If you decide to stay for a bit you can help me.'

Between them they cleared an area round the bed, and Patsy found sheets and a duvet and pillows. When she came back into the room Katy was leaning out of the open window.

'It's so quiet,' she said. 'Just sheep and an owl. Doesn't it bother you, all alone here?'

'No,' Patsy told her honestly. 'It's such a relief to get away from the noise and the smell of exhaust, and...' she stopped, but Katy finished for her.

'And from Dad,' she said. 'You may as well admit it...you led a miserable life for the last few years, all that neurotic business about poisoned food, and always wanting to know exactly where you were going and how long you'd be...to the minute...he used to start ranting if you were even five minutes late.'

'Yes, and from that,' admitted Patsy. For a minute they were both silent, remembering, and then Katy sighed and turned back to face the room.

'Perhaps you are right about Andrew,' she said. 'How do I know what he'd have been like as we got older? He could be pretty funny about some things, like me not being where he expected me to be if he rang, although I was never allowed to enquire about where he'd been.'

'You were both insecure about each other,' Patsy pointed out. 'Not a very good basis for any relationship.'

Together they made the bed and then Patsy went to the door.

'Sleep well,' she said' 'Tomorrow I'll show you the hills.'

CHAPTER SIX

It seemed strange to have another live person in the house. Lying in bed later Patsy was aware that Emrys was restless as well. Doors banged, and a window swung open. She got up to close it, and the cats, coming in for a bite to eat during their night wanderings, went out again quickly, the cat flap banging behind them. Sometime towards dawn the weather changed. The wind began to sigh in the eaves and around the chimneys and a burst of rain roared briefly on the roof and rattled on the windows.

By the time Patsy got up it was raining steadily, the view of the hills blotted out by the mist and the yard running with water. Shrouded in her long mackintosh Patsy fetched David and Goliath in and gave them their breakfast. Eithin Aur and her foal were sheltering with their tails to the bank, but were quite peaceful. Inside the house was quiet; the cats had come in again and settled round the stove, and Emrys seemed to have accepted the situation. Patsy was drinking coffee and reading a two-day-old *Horse and Hound* when Katy came down, dressed in jeans and sweat shirt, and yawning.

'Is it always so noisy at night?' she asked. 'I hardly got to sleep...I suppose it was the wind getting up, but it does make a racket.'

'Yes, it does catch the windows.' Patsy was not going to tell Katy her ghost story. 'It isn't much of a day for riding on the hills, I'm afraid.'

'I don't care.' Katy was restless. 'It isn't as if it was cold. Let's go for a ride...I haven't ridden for ages. Do you mind riding old David?'

It seemed strange to see Katy on Goliath again. Following his broad brown and white bottom out of the yard on the eager David, Patsy remembered hundreds of other rides like this on the Surrey commons, and days at shows, watching Goliath tackle the large coloured fences with an eagerness and agility that his solid shape and suspicious temperament always made so surprising. In deference to the weather Patsy instructed Katy to turn the opposite way to the track which led to the hills, so that they could make a circuit of the sheltered, high banked lanes. The worst of the weather blew over them, catching them in gusts when a gateway or a break in the banks left them unsheltered, and when this happened the horses turned their heads sideways and tilted them to keep the rain out of their eyes and ears.

The warm rain had wakened the scents of the hedgerows to vivid life, earth and green growing things, the sweetness of honeysuckle, and the occasional less sweet smells of manure or death, where some creature had died in the depths of a thick hedge. They disturbed a pair of buzzards feeding on a dead sheep, making them rise into the air with their wild cat cries, and a flock of seagulls dotted a freshly muck-spread field with white as they found food in shelter, away from the storm-stirred sea.

Rounding a bend, they came to one of the few wide grass verges in the district and Katy kicked Goliath forward.

'Let's canter,' she shouted over her shoulder, and Patsy shortened her reins as David broke into an eager canter in pursuit. The canter was exhilarating, wind-driven rain in her face, the pony pulling hard, his short, thick neck arched against the pull on the bit. He loved to be ridden, and he wanted to race. Coming to the end of the verge Katy began to pull up, laughing, and a Land Rover, rounding the bend ahead, braked hard at the sight of them. David piled up behind Goliath, skidding to a stop with his nose in the brown and white horse's tail, and the driver of the Land Rover wound down his window, smiling. Patsy recognised Gareth.

'Hello,' he said. 'Having a bit of a gallop then? I wouldn't have thought it was the weather for riding.'

'Hello Gareth.' Patsy tried to wipe the rain from her spectacles, and peered at him through the smeared glass. 'This is my daughter, Katy, she's here on a visit. Katy, Gareth is my neighbour; his parents own the farm next door.'

'How are you?' said Gareth, in the usual Welsh greeting, and Katy laughed, flushed and exhilarated from the canter, her eyes bright and her fair hair escaping from her riding hat, plastering wetly to her face. Patsy saw dawning interest on Gareth's face and felt a stab of apprehension. In her pre-Andrew days Katy had been quite an expert flirt, and she was showing now that she had not lost the knack.

'So you're a Welsh farmer?' she was saying, sparkling at him. 'I thought they were all old men with sheepdogs and caps. You don't look the part at all.'

'Probably because I'm not a farmer,' Gareth told her. 'It's my Dad who does the farming, I'm a computer man myself, in the dry and away from the toil. I've a day off today, so I'm just running a few errands.'

'How's Bethan?' Patsy decided to get her oar in while there was time. 'You must bring her round for a drink one day.'

'Bethan's away for a bit,' Gareth told her. 'Her Nan in Cardiff has been ill, and she's gone to help out while she gets back on her feet.'

'Oh dear. I hope she'll soon be better.' Patsy decided to get herself and Katy moving again. It was easy to make David restless, with a heel pushed against him on the side away from Gareth. He began to sidle, tossing his head and snorting, and sensing fun Goliath joined in, bouncing up and down and carrying Katy sideways past the Land Rover.

'It looks as if we're moving on,' Katy called back to Gareth. 'Hope I'll see you around.'

Gareth smiled and waved, and the Land Rover moved on. Katy grinned at Patsy.

'He looks nice,' she said. 'Maybe there's hope for Wales yet.'

'He is nice', agreed Patsy. 'But he's spoken for. He and his girl friend, Bethan, are about to name the date, so hands off. Anyway, what about Andrew?'

'Andrew?' Katy took a pull at Goliath, who was trying to start a trotting race. 'Who's Andrew?'

She let Goliath clatter on ahead, and Patsy trotted after her on the eager David. It was nice to see signs of recovery by Katy, but she hoped that her daughter would not begin to create any waves in the local peace.

On the way home they rode past Mack's house, and a loud whinny from behind the hedge announced that Osbourne would like company. Mack appeared from the garage at the noise, and came to lean over the gate and be introduced to Katy.

'He's nice too,' said Katy, as they rode on a few minutes later. 'He's the one you went to dinner with, right?'

'Yes, he and his wife gave me a nice evening,' agreed Patsy. 'And I went to their bar-b-que.'

'I tell you what, you should give a party yourself,' Katy told her. 'Just something simple, in the garden...if it isn't raining.'

'It probably would be.' Patsy was doubtful about this idea. She had never been a very confident hostess, and since her husband had become rather strange, socialising had vanished altogether.

'Then you'd have to move indoors.' Katy was not to be discouraged. 'It isn't as if you didn't have room...I don't suppose you'd invite a huge number.'

Patsy was still doubtful, and she was glad of the diversion when they had to drop into single file to let an enormous lorry loaded with freshly cut timber crawl past them. Katy did not mention the party again then, but as they ate lunch a little later the weather did its local transformation, to which Patsy was growing more accustomed but which astonished Katy. Within twenty minutes the rain stopped, the mist lifted from the hills, the clouds blew away, and the sun lit the landscape with dazzling, golden brilliance. Drops of water flashed from every twig and blade of grass, and the warmth began to raise steam from the drying yard.

'I don't believe it', Katy stated, standing in the back doorway with a cup of coffee in her hand and the cat weaving round her ankles. 'At home, weather like this morning would take half the day to clear.'

'It's because we're so close to the sea,' replied Patsy. 'It is beautiful, isn't it?'

'You know, you'd have a huge chance of good weather for a party.' Katy had not given up the idea. 'Come on, let's have one...no real preparation...just ask everyone to bring something to drink, and we can lay on a few bits to eat and some music. Have you brought the old fairy lights with you?'

'I expect so, somewhere.' Patsy knew when she was beaten. 'All right, but I don't know that many people. We may find no-one will come.'

'I bet they will.' Katy set her cup down on the windowsill. 'Now, what for this afternoon? How about halter-breaking the foal?'

Eithin Aur was good to lead these days, but although Patsy had put the foal slip on her son a few times she had not got any further with him owing to lack of a helper. Having Katy there was certainly a chance not to be missed.

The foal followed his mother into the yard, eager to explore. He trotted about, nosing in corners, chasing one of the kittens, and then coming at a canter when his mother called him. Once in the stable, he sniffed Katy over carefully, and then allowed her to put the slender leather foal slip over his ears. With Patsy gently urging from behind, he was soon walking rather jerkily round the stable. His mother turned a benign head to watch, chewing hay, and Katy scratched his short, woolly neck.

'You said you'd wondered about entering him for one of the agricultural shows,' she said. 'If you do, I'll come and lead him for you. It'd be fun.'

'I'd certainly like to,' Patsy told her. 'You know his sire was a champion at the Royal Welsh?'

'Yes...you said,' Katy agreed. 'You know, maybe Golly could come along too...if there isn't any jumping for him he could do coloured horse or cob or something.'

'He'd enjoy that.' Patsy remembered how Goliath used to enjoy his days at shows, bouncing into the lorry, and then showing off all over the show ground, prancing and snorting and pretending to be a big, scary stallion.

As the evening came on Katy began to grow restless. After eating supper, and switching through the t.v. channels, expressing amazement at the Welsh S4C, she eventually asked to borrow Patsy's car 'to suss out the local night life.'

'I don't think there is much,' Patsy warned her. 'Only the local pubs. They'll be pretty busy with visitors at this time of year.'

'I can go and look.' Katy was determined. 'If I stay in I'll just start fretting about Andrew. I'll take care of the car, I promise.'

'Oh, all right.' Patsy knew that it was no use trying to pin Katy down. Her daughter disappeared upstairs, and twenty minutes later she was back, looking much the same apart from clean jeans and a large, loose pink sweatshirt.

'See you later,' she said, and shortly afterwards Patsy heard the car start and the sound of its engine died away up the lane. Around her the house seemed to settle, the vibrations of Katy's presence fading, and Patsy settled down with the cats and the television with a guilty sigh of relief. She did love Katy, but she had grown used to her peace, and had come to value it.

In spite of her first relief Patsy could not sleep until Katy was home. Lying awake as the clock moved on past midnight she told herself that she was all kinds of fool for doing so. She had thought that the days of staying awake, awaiting the sound of Katy's key in the door or her car in the drive were long over, but it seemed that the habit was not going to leave her so easily. As always the sound of the door and her daughter's soft step on the stairs acted like a soporific, and moments later Patsy was asleep. She did not wake again until the thump of the cat landing on her stomach and a demanding yell from Goliath told her that it was morning, and breakfast time for her four footed dependants.

It was very much later by the time Katy emerged, yawning, from the house. Patsy had finished the chores and was sitting on the large stone in the middle of the yard which acted as seat, mounting block, and rug drying area, enjoying the sun and the peace. It was a fine, still morning, with a high, blue and white sky, and the air above the roofs of the buildings was alive with swooping, banking swallows in pursuit of the myriad of flies and gnats which rose from the warm, damp yard. Patsy wore an old straw hat to keep the midges out of her hair, and her arms, stringy but still muscled where it mattered, were brown and scratched. She wore ancient jeans and a faded blue tee shirt, and her feet were encased in a pair of heavy old work boots. Katy looked at her and laughed.

'You look like a real old farmer,' she said. 'You just need a straw in your mouth.'

'I could soon get one,' said Patsy equably. 'Did you have a good time last night?'

'Not bad at all, for wild West Wales,' Katy told her, 'You were right about the pubs, they really were buzzing. Can we go for a ride now? I want to see those hills a bit closer.'

Patsy had not expected Katy to stay long, but the days passed and she was still there. She stayed in bed late, wandered out to help Patsy in the yard, and to continue with the foal's education, and in the evenings she usually borrowed Patsy's car and went off, coming home late most nights. Patsy fell back into her old routine of reading in bed, dozing and waking, until she finally heard the car bump in over the cattle grid and stop. Telling herself that it was ridiculous, that Katy was a grown woman and not a child, did nothing to stop this. Roads were still dangerous places, more so in a way round here, where many drivers were inexperienced and bends, hills, and blind turns were common. When Katy had been living her own life many miles away, Patsy had been able to accept that it was no longer her responsibility, but now, with her daughter back in the house, this was no longer possible. She never told Katy, and by the time the front door opened her light at the back would be off.

Another thing that Katy's presence had changed was Patsy's consciousness of Emrys. He was still there: she sometimes felt a movement in the air when she came in from outside, and when Katy was out she knew that the house was not empty, but there were no disturbances and no contact. In a way it was a relief, but at the same time Patsy found that she was missing him.

'Ridiculous,' she told herself, 'No-one can miss a ghost.'

But she did, and sometimes she almost resented Katy for disturbing the balance of her new life and home.

'Your girl seems to have settled in,' said Rhiannon one day, when Patsy met her in Tesco. 'Does she not find it lonely at all?'

'She doesn't seem to,' Patsy told her. 'She goes out a lot; I think she's made friends in the district.'

'Still, it's company for you,' said Rhiannon. 'John and I used to wonder would you be all right all alone there.'

'I was, really,' said Patsy. 'Though I was glad to have such good neighbours in you and John and Gareth. How is he? I haven't seen him for a bit. Is Bethan back? He said she'd had to go away.'

'She's still in Cardiff,' Rhiannon told her. 'Her nan still isn't very mobile, but we're hoping she'll be back soon. She'll have to be, or her job will go...she works for the council, they can't do without a secretary for ever.'

'Gareth must miss her,' said Patsy, with faint alarm bells ringing in her head. Just who did Katy see in the evenings?

'Oh, he does,' agreed Rhiannon. 'Working hard, though, he is, out late seeing customers' computers, often now.'

The alarm bells grew louder, but Patsy refused to let them register. Surely Katy hadn't moved that fast, after Andrew?

That afternoon, while they were riding, Patsy tried some gentle inquiries. Had Katy met anyone interesting in the evenings? Did she find it easy to fit in?

Apparently Katy had. West Wales, she declared, was a great place, everyone was friendly, and there were some wonderful characters. There were dedicated conservationists, wealthy weekenders, hippies growing their own cannabis, stuffy retired English and lively young Welsh. And that, Patsy knew, was all the information she was going to get, as she listened to Katy's tale of a man who had rung the police to complain that his neighbour's cows had broken in and eaten his crop of cannabis. The conversation was broken up even more by the usual thunderous arrival of Osbourne and Mack, and soon Patsy was following some way behind on the frantically pulling David as the two horses set off at full speed down the rough track.

Later, while they settled the horses, Katy returned to the subject of Patsy giving a party.

'You owe people,' she insisted. 'Mack and Tabitha, Rhiannon and John, Gareth, Jim the farrier and his wife...and lots of people I've met would come.'

'I suppose so.' Patsy groaned at the thought, but Katy was not going to let her off.

'What about next Saturday?' she said. 'The weather forecast is good for this week. '

There was no getting out of it. Katy was filled with energy, going off to Tesco for basic drinks and food, rooting in the still packed boxes for the fairy lights, hauling the old mower out of the shed and cutting the grass around the house, which was long enough to keep several horses. She also kept Patsy working with her at Hedfa Aur's education, and persuaded Patsy to enter the mare and foal for their section of the Welsh cob classes at Cardigan agricultural show.

'Then you can see just how good a foal you've got,' she said. 'And it'll be fun.'

Patsy did not take much persuading. She too was keen to see how the foal compared with others, and it would be very nice to do something horsey with Katy again.

Katy had also become keen on long rides over the mountain, at first with Patsy or Mack, and then on her own as she became wise to the boggy places and steep drops. She seemed much closer now to the lively, adventurous daughter that Patsy had shared so much with in her youth, and it was great to have her back.

The day of the party arrived, and it looked fine and settled. Patsy, catching some of Katy's enthusiasm, helped with rigging the lights and carrying out the old kitchen table to stand in a corner of the garden. A clean white sheet did duty as a cloth, and Katy stood Patsy's old stereo out on the kitchen windowsill so that the music filled the garden and set the horses trotting round their fields in surprise. When everything was ready Katy disappeared upstairs to take possession of the bathroom, and Patsy made herself a much needed cup of tea while she waited for her turn. Drinking it, she wondered what Emrys would think of a party. Parties had never been his kind of thing, from what Patsy had heard, but so far there had been no evidence of him, disapproving or otherwise.

It did not take Patsy long to have a shower and put on a pair of black trousers and a blue tunic top with some embroidery round the neck. She had not dressed up even to this extent for so long that she felt like a different person as she looked at her reflection in the mirror. Her hair was a bit too long, but she had brushed it well and put a black velvet headband on to keep it out of her eyes, and she even applied a faint trace of eyeshadow and a touch of lipstick. Downstairs again, she heard a car coming down the track, and at the same moment Katy came running down the stairs, a Katy transformed in a pair of bright pink cropped trousers and a very low-cut black top. Her fair hair hung sleek and shining round her face, and her eyes were huge with skilfully applied eyeshadow and darkened lashes.

'You look good,' she told her mother, and Patsy said, 'So do you'. It was more than party clothes, there was a glow about Katy which Patsy had seen before, especially in the early Andrew days. Katy was expecting someone special.

The first arrivals were Mack and Tabitha, and Patsy took them through into the garden and supplied them with drinks.

'This looks great,' said Mack appreciatively, looking round the shadowy garden and the lights just starting to show in the surrounding bushes as the sun sank.

'Yes, Emrys would never recognise it,' agreed Tabitha, and received a quelling look from Mack. Any more was checked by the arrival of the farrier, Jim Gates, and his wife Megan, closely followed by Rhiannon and John. Some young friends of Katy's arrived shortly after them, and Patsy was kept too busy greeting everyone and seeing that they were supplied with drinks to notice when Gareth arrived. The first she saw of him was as part of a group including Katy, all laughing and chattering, and her concern faded a little. Katy was sparkling, certainly, but seemingly just as part of the group. Patsy told herself not to be suspicious. Katy was entitled to some fun after Andrew, and it was good to see her recovery.

As the long dusk descended over the garden, and the hills faded into the blue shadows, the party settled down. People found chairs or perched on the garden wall, Patsy spread the eats out on the table, and moved from group to group, feeling herself relax and lose her first tense shyness. She had never enjoyed being a hostess, but tonight, in these surroundings and with these undemanding people, she began to enjoy herself. She had been accepted into the community more than she had realised, she soon discovered, although she was English and an incomer. She was not one of the wealthy retired who took over houses that could have been sold, more cheaply, to the local young, or one of the considerably resented second-homers. No-one had been keen to buy Bryn Uchaf except her, and she was undemanding and eccentric enough to have been allowed to fit in.

It was almost dark when Patsy, moving on from talking to Rhiannon to see if Jim and Megan had fresh drinks, noticed that Katy was not part of the noisy group of young people who had settled a little apart from the rest. Neither, she was worried to notice, was Gareth. She was looking round, wondering whether to investigate, and deciding that she was really not entitled to interfere, when there was a sudden uproar in the yard, galloping hooves, and a lot of whinnying.

'Sounds as if you've had a breakout,' said Mack, getting to his feet. 'Any help needed?'

'I expect they've just pushed the gate open somehow; I'll have a look.' Patsy did not want everyone swarming out into the yard. It would probably be easier to deal with her horses alone. Putting down the glass that she was holding she went through the little gate into the dark yard, seeing Goliath's flashing white patches and Eithin Aur's tossing blond mane in the shadows. Then the yard lights came on, and she saw Katy in the feed room doorway.

'How did they get out?' Katy demanded. 'The whole lot of them...David's chasing the foal.'

'You catch David. I'll try to get the mare into her stable...the foal will follow.'

Patsy saw Katy head for David, who was snorting and sniffing at the foal as if he wanted to blow him over, as the mare turned to run at him.

'Mind her heels,' Patsy warned Katy, who had grabbed David with a rope round his neck. The mare still wore a headcollar in the field, as she was sometimes wary to catch, and Patsy seized that and turned her towards her stable. The foal soon joined his mother, and Goliath followed Katy and David to stand watching as Katy pushed the little brown pony into his stable.

'Sorted,' she said. 'Can we leave them in for now? Don't want to break up the party.'

'Yes, they can go out later, and I'd better tie the gate,' replied Patsy. 'I can't understand how both their gates could open; I suppose they were rubbing on them or something.'

Or was there another reason? What had Katy been doing in the yard? And where was Gareth? Katy looked very innocent, walking in front of her back to the lights of the party, which were looking brighter now that the last of the light was almost gone, but when Patsy re-joined the party it did not seem quite the same. Deep shadows had gathered, and seemed to be hanging extra thickly around the sides of the house and under the bushes, and some of the older people were starting to glance around, looking a little uncomfortable. Katy was standing by the gate to the yard as Patsy looked back for her, and at that moment all the lights went off, plunging the garden in what seemed for a moment complete darkness. Then the twilight glimmered through, and Patsy heard the murmurs of surprise, and a few laughs. Mack materialised beside her,

'Probably your trip-switch,' he said. 'Shall I take a look? Have you got a torch handy?'

'Just inside,' Patsy told him. 'Thank you, Mack.'

She held the torch for him as he climbed onto a chair to peer at the bank of trip-switches in their box just beside the back door. Sure enough, the main switch was down, and when Mack pushed it back the lights came up again.

'Bit of an over-load,' he said, stepping down. 'Best switch off some of the inside lights for now.'

Patsy did so, and followed Mack back outside. Katy was no longer in sight, and as Patsy looked round to see who needed more drinks the lights went off again. This time the murmur and laughter was louder, and Patsy heard Tabitha say 'I knew he wouldn't like a party...'

It was just what she had been thinking herself, since the ponies escaped, and it seemed that Tabitha was not alone in her opinion. Mack repeated his actions with the trip-switch, but when Patsy went outside again people were starting to make movements towards leaving. Out in the yard a horse was kicking and banging, and Patsy saw Katy back in the garden gateway.

'The mare's making a fuss about something,' she told Patsy rather crossly. 'You'd better have a look.'

'All right, just a moment.' Patsy had to say 'Good night' first to her departing guests. Even the younger ones were heading for their cars, and Rhiannon came up to Patsy.

'Thank you for a lovely evening,' she said. 'John and I really enjoyed it...a bit too much, maybe...I think we'd better get Gareth to run us home...I asked him to keep sober just in case. Now, where is he...?

Katy had overheard. Patsy saw her fade away back into the yard, and when she went round to the front with Rhiannon and John, Gareth was waiting by their Land Rover.

'Good thing I got a lift here, isn't it?' he said cheerfully. 'Come along, my inebriate parents...let's get you home'

It was not long before the last car bumped out over the cattle grid, and Patsy and Katy were left alone.

'That was fun.' Katy seemed quite happy. 'Right Mum, we'd better sort out those crazy horses.'

Don't ask questions, or comment, Patsy decided. If anything is starting with Gareth it may die down if you keep quiet. Surely Bethan must be home soon? As she followed Katy down the yard Patsy did wonder if Rhiannon had noticed anything...she and John did not appear to have had much to drink...but it was a nice way to take Gareth home. If she had, it was more likely that she would influence Gareth than that she herself would have any influence over Katy. And what had upset Emrys...if it was Emrys who had been disturbing things...a party on his patch, or something that had been going on in the barn?

The next few days were peaceful enough. Patsy and Katy worked with the mare and foal, and by now the foal would trot up alone in front of his mother, Katy stepping out so that he did the same, lifting his knees high, tail up and neck arched in true cob fashion. Katy began to talk about breaking Eithin Aur to ride as soon as her foal was weaned, and Patsy agreed that it was a good idea. They were sitting on the stone mounting block in the yard, drinking coffee in the warm sunlight, Patsy in her old jeans and a shabby tee shirt, her old straw hat tilted forward to shield her eyes. Looking at her, Katy began to laugh.

'You look as if you'd grown here,' she told her mother. 'You've been wearing those clothes, or something very like them, ever since I came, except for the party. Haven't you got any other things?'

'Not really, most of my work clothes are pretty worn,' admitted Patsy. 'But so what'? No-one round here from the farms looks very smart.'

'No, but they don't have holes in their trousers,' Katy pointed out. 'Why don't you treat yourself to a day shopping in Carmarthen? I can hang around here, though I don't suppose anything dramatic will happen.'

'I suppose I could,' agreed Patsy. Now that Katy had suggested it, the thought of a day doing something different, such as looking round a small town, seemed quite attractive, and so, two days later, Patsy put on her tidiest pair of trousers and a clean shirt and set off, leaving Katy proposing to clean out the very untidy tack and feed room.

CHAPTER SEVEN

It was a nice day, bright and breezy, and as she drove away from the Preseli hills into the lanes towards Carmarthen Patsy felt quite a sense of adventure. The country here was high, rolling farmland with the familiar small fields of Pembrokeshire, and on a ridge the towering pillars and spinning blades of a wind farm flashed in the sun. Patsy was driving up the last long hill before she would drop down towards the main road when the car's engine suddenly missed, picked up again, and then quietly died. Patsy tried the starter, but got only a click in reply. She was well out in the road, and so she released the handbrake and let the old car run back until she could steer backwards into a handy gateway. She had owned enough oldish cars to know that, when everything died like this, it was likely to be a long holdup, but she got out without much hope to have a look under the bonnet.

As Patsy had expected there was nothing obvious to see. All the leads seemed to be in place, the battery had not fallen out and the fuel gauge showed the tank to be three-quarters-full. Sighing, Patsy perched on the bonnet and fished out her mobile 'phone to call the AA.

There was the usual longish wait and then a tow-truck from a local garage with an AA sign above the cab chugged into sight. After some testing and prodding and listening with an electrical device the mechanic said that he was pretty certain that she needed a new alternator.

'I've got one in stock, back at the garage,' he said. 'I'll be as quick as I can.'

Patsy thanked him, accepting the fact that her trip to Carmarthen had come to an abrupt end.

It took the mechanic about an hour to fetch the part. Patsy climbed over the gate by which she was stopped and sat in the long grass, resigned, and finding the peace and the view of the green and gold patchwork fields and the bare hills beyond quite reasonable compensation for her lost shopping trip. By the time the part was fitted it was too late to go on, and Patsy's enthusiasm for the trip had faded. She turned the old car round and headed back towards the hills. She would have a late lunch in the garden and then bask in the sun and the summer scents.

That pleasant plan was not to happen either. As Patsy drove across the cattle grid into her yard she became aware of a car alarm shrilling away somewhere nearby and the sound of galloping hooves from the field. At the same time, she saw the ladder up against the front of the house with a man dressed only in jeans at the top of it trying to open the bedroom window behind which she saw her daughter's frantic face. As she scrambled out of the car the man looked round. She recognised Gareth.

'Gareth...what...?' Patsy began, starting to realise what was going on as she heard Katy's frantic shouts of 'Mum... I'm locked in, the windows won't open... the door's stuck...the car alarm...'

At that moment the window suddenly swung open, Gareth fell off the ladder and Katy seemed about to scramble out after him. Patsy dashed forward. Gareth had landed in the bushes under the window. In front of him the front door now stood open and the car alarm had stopped.

'Katy...don't jump... the door's open... come down,' Patsy shouted.

For a moment she thought that Katy would ignore her but then her face vanished and a moment later she came flying out of the front door half wrapped in a sheet. Behind her the front door shut with a final, decisive bang. Emrys was showing his disapproval of what had clearly been going on under 'his' roof. Leaning against the car Patsy began to laugh. It really did serve Katy right.

'Mum... stop it, it wasn't funny... first the bedroom door slammed just after Gareth went to turn that alarm off, then the door wouldn't open...and I heard someone laughing in there. Gareth...Gareth said something about Emrys... What's happening?'

'Retribution,' Patsy told her.

Katy's sheet was still slipping and behind her Patsy saw the front door swing open again. She took Katy's arm as Gareth scrambled out of the bushes and started towards his car, parked by the barn.

'I should have known better...I should have known old Emrys wouldn't have it...' Gareth was heading for the barn, zipping his trousers. 'I'm sorry Katy...'

As he reached his car, the hose, which was draped along the front of the buildings on a series of hooks, suddenly came to life, twisting and spitting as it always did when the water was suddenly turned on, and sending a jet of cold water spurting over Katy.

'Ow,' howled Katy, as her sheet fell away and the water soaked her. 'Stop it...go away...help me Mum...'

She threw herself into her mother's arms, and Patsy received a douche of water as well.

'Emrys,' Patsy shouted. 'Stop it...I'll deal with this...' Behind them Gareth's car raced out and clattered over the cattle grid and for a moment nothing changed. The hose continued to spurt and then, as suddenly as it had started, the water was turned off, the hose dropped to the ground, and there was a sudden feeling of stillness. Sobbing hysterically Katy clung to her mother.

'How can you?' she wailed. 'How can you live here...it can't be true...tell me it isn't true.'

'That what isn't true?' Patsy asked her. 'That Gareth's gone off...and that he believes in ghosts...or that it really was a ghost...or that maybe you and Gareth have guilty consciences and imagined things happening, or why they were happening. After all, it was a pretty mean thing to do, wasn't it Katy...coming on strong to Gareth when you knew he had a committed relationship with Bethan, and there was no way you wanted more than a bit of reassurance after Andrew going off...'

'How do you know it was like that?' Katy forgot to be scared in sudden anger. She dropped her arms from her mother and backed off, bristling like an outraged cat. 'I was really keen on Gareth...he's lovely. You don't know anything.'

Behind Katy's back Patsy saw the hose stir and she hastily took Katy's arm.

'Come on,' she said. 'You can't stand about like this...if someone comes I'll never live it down. Go and find some clothes and then we'll have a coffee and talk.'

'Go back in there?' Katy stared at the house in horror. 'No way...I'm not going into that madhouse again...'

'Well, you can't stay here,' Patsy told her. 'Nothing more will happen, I promise. Whatever it was, it's over.'

She glared in the direction of the hose and saw it settle again as though dropped. The feeling of angry tension was fading, the energy dissipating, and she knew that the force that had been Emrys was going, spent. Urging a very reluctant, sheet-shrouded Katy in front of her, Patsy got them both into the hall and closed the front door.

Katy flatly refused to consider staying on. She would not even go up to the spare room to dress and pack, and Patsy brought down clothes and packed up the rest for her.

'Take me to the station, please,' begged Katy, and Patsy knew that she was about to make her trip to Carmarthen after all.

'There may not be a train for hours,' she warned her daughter, 'I'll telephone for the times, and you can wait here. I promise you, nothing more will happen. There's a sort of build up of energy before it does, and it's gone now.'

'Then...then it really is a ghosty?' Katy shivered, looking round.

'I think there probably is,' admitted Patsy. 'It's the man who used to live here...he...well, he killed himself in the yard, he didn't want to have the farm taken away from him, and he still resents other people being here, or living different lives, doing things he doesn't approve of, like...like you and Gareth.'

'But you still stay here?' Katy stared at her. 'How can you?'

'Well, he's never done me any harm.' Patsy was not going to tell Katy that on occasions she felt that Emrys had even helped her. 'He used to breed cobs...I think he's quite pleased to have some back.'

She telephoned rail enquires, and discovered that there was a train in three hours. Katy insisted on going at once.

'I'd rather wait there,' she told Patsy, who gave in. This time the car reached Carmarthen without trouble, and in the station car park Katy gave her mother an uncharacteristic hug.

'I'm really sorry to desert you like this,' she said. 'I was looking forward to leading the foal at Cardigan show...and I've really enjoyed riding Golly again. Maybe I'll come back, if you'll have me, when I can accept this Emrys business.'

'You'll always be welcome, Patsy told her. 'It doesn't matter what you do, Katy, you're still my daughter, and I have liked having you about.'

Driving away from the station Patsy was partly blinded by tears. It had been good to have Katy with her again, and to do the kind of things that they used to do when Katy was younger, but she had to accept, as she thought that she had, that those days were over. But Katy had certainly left her with one practical problem: without her, who would help her to handle Hedfa Aur and his mother at their first show?

Back at the farm, leaning on the gate and watching the mare and foal graze in the long evening shadows, Patsy asked the same question of the empty air.

'It's all very well, being so moralistic and chasing my daughter away,' she said. 'But I don't suppose you've got an answer, have you? Or are you going to lead Hedfa Aur yourself, all scary and invisible? There's one thing, we'd probably win, because you'd empty the ring.'

There was no reply, not even a vibration in the gnat-filled shadows. Emrys's rage had evaporated and with it the energy that had fuelled it. For the moment, anyway, Patsy knew that she was alone.

A few days later Patsy and Goliath were making their way carefully down the stony track to the ford onto the green when Goliath tensed and turned back his ears and a great clattering and slithering behind them warned Patsy that Mack was catching them up, the big horse travelling at his usual headlong speed. Coming alongside, Mack hauled him back to a walk and the two horses exchanged snorts and sniffs.

'Still can't stop the old devil,' Mack told her, fishing in his pocket for a cigarette. 'One glimpse from back there of a friend, and he had to catch you up. That girl of yours not riding him today then?'

'Er, no...Katy had to go home suddenly,' Patsy told him. 'Something...er...happened...'

'Not surprised.' Mack was lighting his cigarette. 'Tabby and I had a bit of a bet on about how long she'd be allowed...I mean...how long she'd stick it here. Not much for the young ones...'

'Yes...things got a bit too much for her.' Patsy knew perfectly well what Tabitha had suspected, and she wasn't going to admit more than that, even to Mack. 'It does leave me with a bit of a problem though...Cardigan show. I was hoping to show the mare and foal...I'd entered them...but I can't manage both of them alone.'

'Want me to give you a hand?' asked Mack. 'I don't mind leading one of them for you.'

'Would you really?' Patsy was pleased. Mack was big and strong enough to help her cope with Eithin Aur if the show atmosphere went to her head.

'I'd enjoy it,' Mack assured her. 'Tabitha always spends hours in the craft tent...give me something to do.'

'Thank you,' Patsy smiled at him. 'Can you come round sometime, and let them get used to you?'

'No time like the present,' replied Mack, and he and Osbourne accompanied Patsy and Goliath home through the cool, shady lanes.

Rather to Patsy's surprise both the mare and foal accepted Mack quite happily. He was firm and quiet, humming peacefully to himself as he led the foal round the yard behind his mother, and he no doubt smelled reassuringly of horses and tobacco. In spite of his wild ways of riding Mack was basically a reassuring sort of person, Patsy decided, as he got back onto the big horse and jogged away towards home.

'So we'll take your Highflyer's grandson to the show after all,' Patsy told the empty yard, and the possibly watching shade of Emrys, but there was no reaction. Either Emrys was no longer there, or Mack's involvement did not disturb him.

***

Mid-summer had come and gone, and the rampant vegetation had seeded, darkened, and become heavy. The hedges were sweet with dog roses and honeysuckle, and the cutter had been round to clear the overgrown grass from the banks so that the lanes now seemed twice as wide. The mare and foal and Goliath were fat and shining, and only David did not seem to have put on as much weight as usual, although he seemed his usual cheerful self. Patsy had his teeth checked by the local horse dentist who found no real sharpness, and she decided that it was merely his age. After all, he was nearing thirty, a very good age for any pony.

'You can't go yet,' she told him, one fresher morning just before Cardigan show. 'Golly and I would miss you far too much.'

David whickered and nuzzled her pocket where he knew the polo mints lived, and Patsy decided that it was no use worrying. Age had to catch up on everyone at some time, and David did not seem any different apart from his weight.

Lying awake in the early hours of the morning of Cardigan show, Patsy heard the weather come in: a rattle of the window, a swish in the trees and bushes round the house, and then the spatter of rain on the glass. Outside, at six o'clock when she went out, the hills were hidden by cloud and the rain was driving across the yard in misty waves, light and thin but very wet. Eithin Aur and her foal had spent the night inside the big stable and the mare greeted Patsy with a shouted demand for breakfast. While Patsy was grooming her a little later, the foal trying to feed at the same time, Mack drove into the yard and climbed out, shrouded in a suit of crackly bright yellow oilskins which sent both ponies diving to the back of the stable.

'It'll clear by lunch time,' he announced. 'Not that Osbourne minds this weather, it keeps the flies away.'

He opened the stable door and crackled in, causing more consternation. Mack did not seem to notice the horrified snorts and stares, as Patsy caught the mare again and led her forward to be tied up once more to the ring from which she had pulled free. He kept talking, lighting a cigarette and telling her a story about Osbourne and the rain, and after a moment Eithin Aur reached out a hesitant nose to sniff him, decided that it was only Mack, and relaxed. Seeing his mother accept this strange yellow monster the foal came forward as well, and soon he was sucking and mouthing the corner of Mack's shiny jacket. Patsy decided that all would be well...no doubt Mack would unveil the clothes in which he would show the foal when they arrived at the scene.

Cardigan show was held in several high, recently cut hay fields, the land falling away towards the sea, with magnificent views of the bay and the Tivy estuary, still veiled in rain at the time that Patsy joined the queue of lorries, horse boxes, and cars waiting to go into the show ground. The parking field was already crowded with horse transport of every kind; the other livestock, following DEFRA regulations, had separate parking. Unloading from the horse transport were equines of every sort, from massive Shires, already decorated with ribbons and brasses, to elegant Arabs and tiny Shetlands, There were many fiery little Welsh Mountain ponies, and of course, the cobs, youngstock, mares, and magnificent, hard-muscled, shining stallions. Looking at one of these, prancing past in his stallion tack, knees lifted high, eyes blazing with pride and challenge, Patsy was able to understand even more how Emrys must have felt at having to lose his beloved Highflyer. These cobs were personalities, line-bred for generations, the very spirit of old Wales, the stuff of legend, and the lives and loves of their once wild, and now unwillingly tamed, traditional Welshmen.

'You'll need to keep hold of your mare, with those boys around,' said Mack, as they got out of the lorry, and Patsy knew that he was right.

Eithin Aur came out of the lorry with a bound that almost swept Patsy off her feet, her foal scurrying behind her with Mack holding on tight. He had now shed his oilskins, and was smart in cords and hacking jacket. At the bottom of the ramp Eithin Aur stopped dead and uttered a mighty screech to announce her arrival. Then she bounded forward, was brought up short by the halter, and swung round Patsy in a wild circle, head and tail high and nostrils wide. Her eyes flared with excitement, and for a moment Patsy thought that she was going to lose her hold, but then the foal crowded close to her flank, and Eithin Aur remembered her responsibilities. She turned her head to nuzzle her baby closer, and Patsy led her round into the shelter of the side of the horsebox. The rain was still drifting across the field in waves but there was a brightness about it now, and from past experience Patsy knew that it would very soon clear,

The judging of the section D cobs was already under way, and the class for mares with foal at foot would be next. Eithin Aur was shaking with excitement, and as the first of the mares and foals went past them on the way to the ring she shrieked and made a dive to follow them. Mack, close by, grabbed the rope just in time.

'Best let me lead her,' he said. 'She'll be too strong for you in the ring...this little fellow's more your weight.'

It made sense. Patsy handed the mare to Mack with relief, and they started towards the gap in the hedge which led through into the main show field. The foal trotted beside Patsy, close to his mother's tail, ears pricked, his whole little body tense with excitement.

In the manner of most agricultural shows there was one huge ring, surrounded by benches and cars, and divided into four smaller rings. There was show jumping going on in one, palomino horses in hand in another, Shetland ponies in a third, and the cobs in the fourth, which, luckily for Patsy, was the closest one to the walkway from the box park. Beyond the benches and the cars was the rest of the show, huge marquees for flowers and crafts, displays of massive farm machinery, trade stands selling everything imaginable from saddlery to reproduction furniture, catering stalls, donkey rides, even a miniature railway. Mack was holding on tight to the mare's halter rope while she dived and shied and pulled, while beside Patsy the foal squeaked and went up on his hind legs. Then they were in the ring, walking round the slightly calmer green space behind other mares and foals, while the judge took a first critical look.

There were eight mares and foals in the ring. The judge called them in to stand in line while each mare in turn was trotted past him, the foals waiting for their mothers to return. Eithin Aur was having none of that. There was no way she was going to leave her baby in the midst of this chaos: anything might happen to him. She reared and swung back to him, hauling Mack round with her, and in the end the judge said, 'Bring the foal too.'

With her baby beside her the mare did consent to trot up, but she was wild and uneven, stopping and starting, although Hedfa Aur arched his baby neck, stuck his little flag of a tail in the air, and stepped out. The judge laughed.

'Someone has the right idea, anyway,' he said.

There were only four rosettes, and although Eithin Aur was called into line sixth she was not placed.

'A very nice mare, but we couldn't judge her properly,' the judge told Patsy and Mack.

Foals were judged separately, and this time Mack held on tight to the mare, forcing her to stay in place while Patsy ran up with the foal. Hedffa Aur loved it. 'Look at me,' said his pricked ears and arched neck. He lifted his knees high in real cob action, finishing with a leap and a squeal as he reached the end of the ring. This time there was no hesitation; he was called in first.

'I'd be surprised if you haven't got a champion in the making there,' the judge told Patsy. 'Highflyer stock, is he? Oh yes, I can see it in him. Good luck with him. I hope to see you both again.'

'That was really well done,' Mack told Patsy, when they were back in the comparative calm of the box park. 'Old Emrys would be really chuffed.'

'It's wonderful.' Patsy felt on a real high. 'I never really believed he was that good.'

'Royal Welsh next year.' Mack was lighting a cigarette, Eithin Aur, calmer now, pulling at the grass. 'He'll be weaned by then, no need for this wild woman to go with him.'

It was an exciting prospect. They loaded the ponies back into the lorry, shutting them in safely, Eithin Aur with a net of hay, and Patsy went to collect her prize. The cob stallions were in the ring now, and she paused to watch. Each in turn, they were run past the judge by their handler, many of them men, who wore dark trousers and white running shoes and strode out in time with their cobs. Their knee action matched that of their charges, and it made an electrifying display. There was much applause, and the winner was called in, a perspiring young farmer with a shining black cob, an animal made of muscular curves, neck, body, quarters, flowing mane and tail, and flashing white socks. Watching the cob handlers, seeing the blazing pride and the fierce competitiveness of these normally quiet, private men Patsy felt better able to understand what had driven Emrys, and how bitter it would have been to him to have to give up his champion. No wonder that even now his pride would not easily accept a replacement, a 'second best'. But perhaps Highflyer's grandson would not be a second best, but an equal or even more than his famous ancestor.

Waiting in line in the tent for her prize Patsy was spoken to by an elderly Welshman, gnarled and bent, dressed in his best suit and cap and leaning on a stick.

'So you're the lady with the Highflyer colt?' he said. 'You'll be living in Emrys's old place, then? What would he be thinking of this, I wonder? You'll know about the boy, won't you?'

'Yes, I do know about Emrys,' agreed Patsy. 'I hope he'd be pleased.'

'Hard to say, very hard,' said the old man. 'Fair play, you've done a good job with the foal...it should please the boy, but there was no telling with Emrys.'

There was a cup for the best foal, as well as a rosette and an envelope containing a few pounds. On the way home in the lorry Mack picked up the cup to examine the names of previous winners engraved on it.

'Ha', he exclaimed. 'Thought so. This cup has been to your house before...Emrys Jones, Bryn Uchaf Highflyer...eight years back.'

'Has it?' Patsy was not surprised. But would its return be welcome, she wondered, as the lorry crept down the lane to the farm gate.

Mack helped her to unload the ponies, and refused her offer of coffee.

'Tabitha will be home by now,' he said. 'She'll have bought plants at the show...my afternoon will be in the garden, putting them in.'

'Thank you very much for helping,' Patsy said sincerely. 'I couldn't possibly have managed them without you.'

'I enjoyed it,' Mack assured her. 'Maybe we can repeat it at the Royal Welsh next year if that girl of yours doesn't come back.'

The clouds had broken as they left the show, and the sun was out as Patsy collected the rosette and cup from the lorry. Taking a deep breath she carried them into the house. What sort of reaction would they get? she wondered.

Patsy was prepared for banging doors and opening windows, things falling down, or even some sign of pleasure. What she wasn't prepared for was...nothing. There was no reaction, no feeling of presence, no sense of Emrys at all. The cats stretched and yawned around the stove, and the mother cat decided that the weather had improved enough to venture out. Patsy made room on the dresser and set the cup in pride of place with the rosette hooked onto it.

'Aren't you pleased?' she asked the empty air. 'Highflyer's grandson...a winner, and a great future. Surely that must help to make things right?'

There was no reaction, and Patsy knew with a ridiculous sense of disappointment that there was nothing and no-one there.

CHAPTER EIGHT

The days following the show seemed something of an anticlimax. The tourist season was in full swing, the roads busy and the beaches crowded. It was impossible to park in the smaller towns, and the queues in Tesco stretched back down the aisles. The weather became hot, and the lower slopes of the hills swarmed with horse flies. Out riding Patsy learned to avoid the B roads and to be on the alert round the lanes for cars travelling too fast as they searched for places of interest, such as the prehistoric Pentre Ifan tomb. She visited this herself one day as evening came on, a very ancient place, three standing stones topped by a huge capstone at a point that commanded a magnificent view of the woods and fields stretching down to the sea. In spite of the two hippies on their knees beside it, beaded heads bent in still contemplation, Patsy was struck by the utter stillness of the place, the enormous sense of the past, and the briefness of life against the hugeness of time. It was a briefness that was to come back to her a few days later when she went out to the horses one morning and found David standing in the centre of his field, covered in dust and looking anxious. Goliath was grazing nearby, but keeping an eye on his friend, as Patsy led him gently towards the gate. He was still loosing weight, and she knew sadly that age was at last catching up with him.

'Have you got a pain?' she asked the old pony, as he stood in his stable, and he nuzzled her half-heartedly. A slice of carrot was accepted, but without his usual eagerness. Patsy went indoors and telephoned the vet.

Simon soon arrived, and checked David over carefully. The pony was still subdued, but he did not seem really uncomfortable, and Simon shook his head.

'There's nothing much to find now,' he said.' It could have been a touch of colic. You could try worming him in a day or so, if he's settled down, but he's a good age, isn't he?'

'Heading for thirty', admitted Patsy, and Simon pulled a face.

'It is a time when things start to break down,' he said. 'I'll give you some Bute to give him if he seems uncomfortable, and call me if it's anything more.'

Patsy left the horses in for the rest of the day, out of the flies and the hot sun, and when she turned them out that evening David seemed back to his usual self. He went off to graze with Goliath, and when Patsy came out to look at them in the moonlight later he seemed quite happy. She determined not to worry too much...some ponies lived much longer than thirty, so why not David?

The pony seemed fine for the rest of the week. The weather turned cooler, and August bank holiday dawned. Patsy was sweeping the yard when Rhiannon's Land Rover rattled over the cattle grid into the yard. Patsy was pleased to see her. She and John had been very busy on the farm recently, with hay and silage to cut, sheep to dip and shear and move around, and a new barn being built. Patsy also felt a lingering guilt over Katy and Gareth, and hoped that Rhiannon did not hold it against her, if she really knew about it.

'John and me were wondering, do you know about the firework display in Newport tonight?' Rhiannon asked Patsy, when they were indoors having a cup of coffee. 'It's a great thing to see, especially from the big beach. We're going down, if you'd like to come. We haven't seen much of you lately.'

Patsy accepted with pleasure. It would be good to have an evening out, and it was nice to know that Rhiannon was not upset about Katy and Gareth. She would ask after him now, to make sure.

'Gareth?' Rhiannon's face changed; she suddenly did look upset. 'Oh, he's well, but we've all been disappointed there. Bethan broke off the engagement...met someone else in Cardiff, didn't she? A great shame, I'm thinking, but there, maybe if she wasn't quite satisfied it was for the best.'

So Katy hadn't done the harm Patsy had feared. She felt guilty now about her daughter...and Emrys. What had happened that day? Was there any way in which her dismay over Katy's flirtation could have caused the strange scene?

'But I wasn't even here when it started,' Patsy remembered. 'No, there couldn't have been anything like that.'

'I am sorry,' she told Rhiannon sincerely. 'I thought they made a really nice couple. Is Gareth very upset?'

'Not so bad now,' Rhiannon told her. 'He's off on a course soon that will give him a break...time to forget a bit, maybe.'

'I'm sure he'll find someone else,' Patsy told her. 'Girls aren't going to let a boy like Gareth get away from them for ever.'

'I'm sure that's right,' agreed Rhiannon. 'Well, I must get back to the farm...we'll pick you up, then, about six thirty.'

'I'll look forward to it,' Patsy assured her.

When Rhiannon had gone Patsy rinsed the cups, and paused in the living room. The stove, still alight in spite of the warm weather, was shut right down, just enough to warm the cooler early mornings and offer a warm oven to crisp up a bread roll or heat a pie. It made soft clicking sounds, and close to the window a sparrow was chirruping. Patsy felt alone, but she was never certain if she was.

'You see?' she asked softly. 'It wasn't so wrong, was it? There was never any future to break up...if you'd left well alone things would have been nicely sorted out anyway.'

There was no reaction, but all the same Patsy had a feeling that her words had been heard.

The great sweep of Newport Beach was alive with crowds arriving to watch the display by the time Patsy, Rhiannon, and John had found somewhere to park the Land Rover and had walked the rest of the way. The tide was well out, and the wet sand gleamed in the dusk. The calm sea was a half-heard background, murmuring up the beach, as they walked with the cheerful crowd towards the Nevern estuary and the harbour wall on the other side, along which the display would be held. There were many temporary camps and barb-queues set up along the edge of the sand dunes, but at the moment the coming display drew everyone to the best view point. Behind the harbour the softly painted old houses were fading into the dusk, lights coming on in windows, and behind them the hill went up to the castle, and the dark, rock-crowned bulk of Carningli beyond.

The display began with a deep, stomach-shaking boom, and the first fireworks spread in a great starburst across the sky. Feeling more at peace than she had for some time, Patsy settled down to watch.

Later, back home, Patsy went out to the fields to check the horses. The night was very still and a mist was rising, lying waist deep, so that the horses seemed afloat, legless. Only the foal's head and ears were visible above it, as he gazed at her from beside his mother, and as Patsy walked towards the two old horses, rabbits scurried away, small dark shapes hopping in and out of the mist patches. There was a three-quarter moon making the mist luminous, and Patsy felt a magical otherness about the night...a sense of being close to other dimensions. David was standing close to Goliath, as he had begun to do lately, not grazing like his friend, and as she ran her hand over him Patsy could feel his ribs and backbone where the comfortable covering of fat had dropped away. He seemed quite peaceful, though, accepting a polo mint and sniffing Patsy's pockets for more. Partly reassured, Patsy patted him and turned back towards her house, floating above the mist, strangely lit by the moon, the lighted downstairs window orange glowing hazily. Patsy half expected to see Emrys standing there, it was that kind of night, but there was nothing, only the cats, slipping shadowlike out of the mist to rub round her ankles as she stepped into the porch. Yawning, Patsy fed them, and then made her way upstairs to bed.

Patsy woke late the next morning, coming suddenly out of a dream to hear Goliath's roar. Going outside a few minutes later she knew at once that something was wrong. Goliath was by the gate, pawing the ground and shouting, and casting agitated glances over his shoulder. Looking beyond him Patsy saw a brown heap on the ground, beside the hedge where the two old ponies often spent their nights.

'David.' Patsy ran across the field, leaving Goliath staring after her. The old brown pony was still alive, but his nostrils were blown wide and he was gasping for breath. His eyes were unfocussed, concentrating on the pain inside him, and Patsy turned to run back to the house and the telephone.

Simon promised to be with her inside ten minutes, and Patsy seized a rug from the rack in the tack room and ran back to David. Goliath had not left the gate and the mare and foal were grazing as far away as possible.

Kneeling down, Patsy spread the rug over David as gently as possible and remained beside him, tears blinding her as she stroked his sweat-soaked neck. Memories crowded in...David and Katy winning a hunter trial in the pouring rain, the pony galloping bright-eyed and full of going through the finish when so many had trotted in exhausted...David coming to meet her in his field, happy and confident, David out in the field on a winter night, out in the field in the snow, as warm as a radiator under the white coating, and David on the day she had first met Mack, trotting off so happily to meet the wild ponies.

'Oh David...don't go,' she whispered to him, but she knew it was no use. David was struggling to raise his head, his eyes suddenly focussed and aware, and as she put her arm under his head he whinnied, a call ahead into the unknown darkness descending on him. Then his head went heavy on Patsy's arm and the laboured breathing went out on a long, rattling sigh. She was bent over him, stroking him and whispering her goodbyes, when she felt a hand on her shoulder and Simon said, 'I'm sorry, I came as fast as I could.'

'I should have got up earlier, but he didn't seem bad last night.' Patsy got shakily to her feet.

'You can never predict what will happen when they reach this age,' Simon told her. 'I've seen them rally and carry on for months. I'll 'phone the right people for you: they'll fetch him pretty quickly.'

'I'd like to bury him here,' Patsy told him. 'I...I know you aren't supposed to, but surely...an old pet? Can I telephone my neighbours?'

Simon agreed, assuring her that he was not going to rush off and report her, and Patsy went sadly indoors to telephone Rhiannon.

'Oh Patsy, I am sorry, I know how hard it is when the old favourites go.' Rhiannon sounded upset. 'Of course John will come, don't worry about that old ministry and its regulations.'

Outside again Patsy found that Simon had put Goliath into his stable.

'He was fretting,' he told her. 'Best if he doesn't see any more.'

'What do you think it was?' Patsy asked him.

'Probably an internal haemorrhage,' said Simon. 'I suspect he had a growth; there was nothing we could have done at his age.'

He drove off after telling Patsy to let him know if she had any problems about disposal and Patsy fetched hay and feed for Goliath, who was standing very quietly at the back of his stable. Eithin Aur came to her gate as well at the sound of the feed bins, and Patsy brought her and the foal into their stable as well. Then she went back to David.

She was sitting beside him, waiting and remembering, when she heard the tractor drive into the yard and John and Rhiannon came across the field to her.

'Come along in,' Rhiannon told her. 'John will see to it, he'll find a good spot that won't upset the ministry too much if they do find out. You don't want to watch, not nice, it won't be.'

'Thank you.' Patsy gave David a last gentle touch. 'Take...take care of him.'

'I will,' John promised, and Patsy let Rhiannon lead her across the field, an arm round her shoulders. Later, when the job was done and Rhiannon and John had gone, Patsy went back outside. Goliath was watching her from his stable, his eyes wide and anxious, and he greeted her with his usual deep roar. Patsy took a rope from the tack room and clipped it onto his headcollar.

'Let's go together,' she said. 'You need to say goodbye as well.'

Goliath crowded out of the stable, and Patsy led him through the gate into his field. There was another gate on the far side, leading into a patch of rough ground before the land dropped away into the wood. The marks of the tractors wheels led through this gate, and the ground had been freshly dug and smoothed flat. It was a good place, sheltered and quiet, surrounded by long grass and bracken, and the tall spikes of foxgloves. In spring it would be a mass of wild flowers, and the ground would not become waterlogged in the winter.

Snorting, Goliath followed Patsy through the gate and lowered his head to sniff the freshly dug ground.

'He's here,' Patsy told him. 'Your friend is here. His body will always be here. I hope his spirit has found green fields and friends where it's gone, even if he has had to leave you behind.'

Goliath snorted and began to paw the ground. Then he raised his head and whinnied, long and loud, a sound quite unlike his usual roar, and then he stood stiff, ears pricked, as though listening. There was no reply, only the sound of bees in the foxgloves and a bird singing close by. Her eyes full of tears, Patsy said, 'He's really gone, Golly. Go to rest in peace, David, we...we'll never forget you.'

Then she turned Goliath and he came with her quite willingly back to his stable.

A little later Patsy had to telephone Katy to break the news, and as she had expected, Katy was very upset.

'I wish I'd been there,' she said. 'Poor little David. I...I had so much fun with him and he was always such a good little pony.'

'I wish you'd been here as well,' Patsy told her. 'Why don't you come down and visit again? Nothing odd has happened since you left.'

'I...I don't know...perhaps sometime.' Katy was backing off. 'Maybe we could fix something at Christmas...you could even visit me. Surely someone would look after the horses?'

'I'll think about it', Patsy told her. Ringing off, she felt suddenly angry.

'Think what you've done', she told the air, and the possible listener. 'Scared my girl away for good, and for what? What do you think you are, interfering in the lives of people who still have a way to go, and some happiness to find. It may be too late for you, but what you've done isn't fair.'

Unexpectedly there was a stir in the air, and the back door suddenly swung open. Startled, Patsy span round in time to see it slam shut. It seemed that her angry outburst had made a connection.

Next day, rather anxiously, Patsy turned Goliath, who was very subdued, out with Eithin Aur and the foal. The mare was very defensive at first, sniffing noses with Goliath and squealing loudly, and very careful to keep herself between him and her baby, but when

Goliath showed little interest, and began to graze a little apart, she relaxed, and by lunch time all three were grazing together, tails to the rising westerly wind which was blowing in from the sea. It was September, autumn was already touching the leaves, the days were shortening, and Patsy knew that the testing time for her in this new life was fast approaching.

It took time. At first September was a golden month: some days were stormy, but many more were quiet and mellow, with the hills turning golden-brown and the streams growing wider as the increased rainfall high up swelled them. It was time to wean Hedfa Aur, and at Mack's suggestion Patsy took the mare to stay with Osbourne while they became used to the separation, and her milk dried up. At first, Mack reported, she ran round screaming while Osbourne watched in puzzled amazement, but it did not take long for her to settle. At Bryn Uchaf, Hedfa Aur called for his mother for a day, but he had the reassuring solidity of Goliath for company, and he was soon content with that. Goliath was the perfect uncle, content to stand head to tail if the flies were bad, or to lend his bulk as shelter from the wind, and yet he was still bright enough to run and play for a time when Hedfa Aur demanded it.

Katy telephoned her mother more regularly now, and chatted, but she still would not come and visit. There was something almost secretive about her which made Patsy suspect a new boyfriend, and she hoped that this time the relationship would be happier than the one her daughter had had with Andrew. Rhiannon called in when she was passing Patsy's drive, and reported that Gareth had stayed away on a long course, and Patsy knew that her friend was still regretting the end of her hopes for him and Bethan.

'It would have settled him, see, kept him near us, we'd hoped,' she told Patsy. 'But there, it wasn't to be. '

'It would be nice to have our children stay around,' agreed Patsy. 'But they have their own lives, and the less we try to interfere the better.'

Out in the yard Rhiannon nodded towards the telephone wires running above the yard. They were lined with swallows, while above their heads many more darted and swooped.

'Winter's coming,' she said. 'They're starting to gather...not so long now before they're off to the sun.'

It was rather a daunting thought. Patsy had always known that her first winter at Bryn Uchaf would be her real testing time, and as Rhiannon drove out she looked up at the graceful blue and white birds with their flash of red.

'You probably have more sense than most of us humans,' she told them. 'Sun and warmth and light winds...that's where you're heading. I hope you all get there safely.'

How would she be feeling by the time they returned, she wondered. Suddenly it seemed a long time until next spring.

Coming out of the house two days later Patsy was struck by the stillness in the yard. There was no movement above her, or in and out of the stables and sheds, and the sky above, blue and clear but with a sharp chill this morning, was empty, apart from a pair of jackdaws heading for the chimney. The swallows had gone, and when she fetched Goliath in for his breakfast and his few hours of peace in his stable she noticed how much his brown and white coat had thickened. Eithin Aur was back now, and she, the foal, and Goliath had become a contented threesome, There was still plenty of grass in the fields, but Patsy had laid in a good store of hay when John cut his fields, and there was a comfortable feeling of plenty as she passed the hay shed with its sweet summer scent, bulging with still green bales.

There was a stormy sunset that evening: streaks of dark cloud were rising from the west, stained vivid red as the sun went down below them, and a great fan of grey cloud was spreading in front of them. The weather forecast warned of strong winds, and just after midnight the first strong gust rattled the windows. By morning it was blowing hard, driving sheets of grey rain across the fields and blotting out the hills. All the cats were clustered on or in front of the stove, and outside Goliath was at the gate, shouting that he was being neglected, this was no weather for a horse. The mare and foal were grazing in the shelter of the banks, unworried, but Goliath came shouldering into his stable and almost knocked Patsy over as he began to rub his large, wet body against the walls. Patsy fed him and put some hay out for Eithin Aur and her son, and then retreated to the warmth of the back room. There would be no sudden transformation to sunlight and blue sky today, she suspected.

The weather that day set the tone for most of the coming weeks. Day after day Patsy awoke to winds which never seemed to drop, and which sent the rain horizontally across her fields. Water poured down the yard, swelling the stream, which was soon running well above its normal banks, although still well below the level of the yard, which had obviously been carefully sited. Mack sent Osbourne to stay at the local riding school while he and Tabitha went to visit relations in England for an extended stay, and Patsy went days without seeing another soul unless she splashed out in her car to the shops. She discovered that she did not really mind. She had books to read, plenty of chores to be done, and she began to re-decorate the very shabby front room, which she used less and less as the weather deepened. It was much more comfortable in the back room with the cats and the murmuring stove. And there was Emrys. Although there were no spectacular outbursts Patsy was again conscious that she was not entirely alone at Bryn Uchaf. There were doors that quietly swung open, changes in the atmosphere, and sudden awakenings and stares into space by the cats. It was almost comforting, until one night Patsy was awoken by the smell of smoke, and the crash of the cat flap as several cats bundled out in line. She had smoke alarms fitted both in the hall and on the landing, but they had not gone off.

Going out onto the landing Patsy found the air thick with smoke, rising from the stairwell. Grabbing a towel from the bathroom she hastily wetted it, and holding it over her nose and mouth, she stumbled downstairs. The smoke was coming from in front of the stove, and Patsy could see the flicker of a small flame from the direction of the carpet runner she had in front of the Rayburn. She dived into the kitchen, grabbed the washing up bowl, and filled it with water. Rushing back towards the stove she threw the water over the burning carpet. It took several bowls full, but at last the smouldering fire was out, and she was able to see that the door of the firebox on the stove was open, and some of the carefully stoked up fire had fallen out.

With the back and front doors, and all the windows, open to disperse the smoke, Patsy wrapped herself in her thickest jacket and found that she was shaking, partly from shock and partly from the bitter wind which swept into the house.

'I can't have latched it properly,' she thought, but she knew that she had. She always double-checked that door before leaving it for the night. And if she hadn't made a mistake, how had it opened?

'You wouldn't...would you?' she asked the smoky air. 'You wouldn't burn Bryn Uchaf down. Why? What is it?'

The front door slammed, perhaps on a stronger gust of wind, and then the back door did the same. Patsy knew that she had her answer.

'You're trapped, aren't you?' she whispered. 'You can't leave here, but perhaps, if it wasn't here, you could. Is that it?'

There was no response, but Patsy was sure that she was right.

'Surely it wouldn't work?' she asked. 'It isn't just the house that ties you, surely? You loved the land even more...What can I do to help? Is there anything?'

'Come with me.' The words were not spoken; they were in the air, in Patsy's head, in the gusts of wind.

'No.' Patsy was alarmed. Had she really heard that? 'No...that isn't the way...I can't come, not...not yet...'

The wind swept through the house harder, forcing the last of the smoke out through the open windows, and Patsy shivered. She was dreaming, and in shock. Of course she hadn't heard anything. It was time to fill herself a hot water bottle and go back to bed.

Next morning the living room smelled of burned carpet and the floor was squelching wet. The stove was still burning, and the cats perched on the top and on chairs, looking hurt. Patsy decided that it must have been nothing but her own carelessness; she must have left that door off the catch. She fed the horses and then got busy mopping up, and throwing out the ruined wool runner. The piece of sisal matting that usually went by the door could replace it until she next went into town.

The weather was better today, dry and bright, but cold, with a brisk northerly wind sweeping the last lingering leaves from the trees. Patsy saddled Goliath and went for a ride round the quiet, sheltered lanes. It would be Christmas in a couple of weeks: she must buy a few presents and organise her own Christmas day. Katy, when asked again if she would consider coming down, had been very cagey, although she had begged her mother to visit her instead. Patsy knew that she could not ask Rhiannon or anyone else to take on her horses, keep the stove burning in case of frost, and feed the cats over the Christmas period. She would have to settle for spending it alone. It wasn't something that really bothered her, Christmas since Katy had been grown up had never been a major thrill in any case. Now, hacking towards home with the cold wind hitting Goliath and her in sharp gusts as they passed the gateways, and the bare hills sharp against the pale blue and white sky, Patsy decided that it could even be a cosy experience on her own.

Presents were fairly straightforward. A top, black and low cut, two CDs , and a book for Katy, a bottle of good wine and a nice indoor plant for John and Rhiannon, book tokens for two rarely seen nieces by marriage living in Manchester and Dundee, and a book she had wanted for herself: these were all that was needed. Struggling through the crowd in Haverfordwest was quite enough Christmas shopping experience for Patsy anyway, and even Cardigan and pretty little Newport were heaving with shoppers and visitors. Food would be simple enough: one hectic visit to Tescos would see to that. Patsy turned her attention to decorating Bryn Uchaf.

There was holly in plenty in Patsy's own wood, where the stream flowed wide and fast along the bottom of the ravine the trees grew down. There was a strong smell of foxes, but the large badger earth in the hillside looked untidy and unused, with dead leaves, and Patsy knew that the badgers were asleep for the winter, deep under the ground. She cut several branches of holly and set off back across the fields, Goliath and the foal coming over to sniff and stare curiously at her burden, while Eithin Aur watched more doubtfully from a distance. She would never have quite the confidence of the more domesticated ponies, and as she went through the gate into the yard Patsy wondered, not for the first time, what to do with her next. She should be broken to ride, but that would mean sending her away and paying quite a lot for the job. It was not something that Patsy wanted to tackle, and in any case she would need help.

'If you hadn't scared Katy away she would have helped me,' she told Emrys, as she walked across the yard, and then stopped herself short. She really must not get into the habit of talking to ghosts, or to herself.

The living room was the perfect setting for Christmas decorations, with the wood panelling shielding the door and boxing in the stairs, the beams in the ceiling, and the wooden shelf above the Rayburn alcove. The mother cat and one of her kittens perched on the stove, watching in amazement as Patsy stood on a chair to fix holly and tinsel, brought from her old home, to the shelf, and wound strings of tinsel around the pillars on the front of her old wooden dresser.

'I'll have to get a tree,' Patsy decided, carried away, as she studied the final effect. 'It'd look so right in the alcove under the stairs.'

There were no fir trees in her wood, so it would mean a trip out. There were Christmas trees for sale on several local farms, and Patsy set out on her quest. She was loading a small tree into the back of her car beside the Haverfordwest road when Rhiannon's Land Rover drew up beside her.

'Getting ready for the big day, I see,' she said. 'Is your girl coming down to visit you?'

'Er, no...she's got something on at home.' Patsy knew that Rhiannon had her suspicions about Katy's sudden departure, and non-reappearance, but she was not going to explain.

'So you'll be all on your own then?' asked Rhiannon. 'John and I were wondering: how would you like to come to us for dinner? Home-raised turkey, it'll be, and John's parents will be with us, but they're easy. We won't like to think of you all alone.'

'It's very, very kind of you, but won't I be intruding?' Patsy was touched and tempted, but she did not want to be invited purely out of pity.

'Not at all,' Rhiannon told her convincingly. 'John's parents are easy, as I said, but they're not young, and we all know each other too well. Lighten things, having you would, we'd really be pleased if you came.'

'Well, I would love to.' Patsy had wondered how she would feel entirely on her own all Christmas. 'Thank you very much.'

'I'm really glad you agreed,' Rhiannon told her. 'We'll see you about one o'clock, then, we'll be well between milkings for the meal by then.'

She drove on, and Patsy finished loading her tree and followed her towards home. It would certainly be better for her to go to Rhiannon's she knew, than to spend the day talking to Emrys.

The little tree fitted perfectly in the space beneath the stairs, the dark green branches set off by the dark wood above it. Patsy had found her old Christmas tree lights, and she twined them around it, finishing it off with garlands of silver and gold tinsel. When she switched on the lights the little tree glowed, softly bright and full of memories of past Christmases, when Katy was small and would stand staring at similar trees with her eyes full of magic. A wave of nostalgia swept over Patsy, and she felt her eyes prick, and yet not all of those Christmases had been happy, with Richard ill and difficult, full of unfounded suspicions of everyone and everything. All the same, Patsy would have welcomed the prospect of Katy's company this year.

'That's another thing you've spoiled,' she said aloud, to the possibly listening shade, and stopped herself short. It really was a good thing she had been invited to Rhiannon's.

Christmas day at John and Rhiannon's revolved around milking times and feeding times, but it was bright and warm and there was plenty of Christmas cheer. John's parents were very elderly, but spry, and John's father insisted on teaching Patsy the right phrases for Christmas in Welsh. There was a home-reared turkey for dinner, and a tree cut from the wood by the farm filled the room with the scent of pine.

The meal over, they settled around the fire with coffee and brandy, and John's father raised his glass to Patsy.

'Time to drink to the incomer,' he said. 'Brave, she is, taking on that place of Emrys's. May the boy let her settle.'

'Dad...' began Rhiannon, but the old man cut her short.

'I would say she knows what I'm meaning,' he said. 'Never one to welcome any woman, was Emrys, thanks to that fierce old mother of his. Never even liked Christmas much, did she? If there were dragons in Wales that was one of them. A good manager, mind, it was only after she went that Emrys had to start selling off bits of the land to keep going.'

'John bought a parcel of it himself, didn't you, lad?' put in John's mother.

'The south field,' admitted John. Rhiannon, who was looking troubled, stood up.

'That's like enough about old troubles,' she said. 'Christmas, it is. Now, more coffee, Patsy, and a hot mince pie? I'm sure you've room left.'

It was dark well before Patsy left John and his father starting the milking and drove herself home, carefully after her share of the wine. She had left the porch light on, as she usually did if she was not expecting to be back before dark, but to her surprise the house and yard were in darkness. Goliath greeted the sound of her car with a roar of welcome, and as she got out of the car two cats materialised from the shadows to twine round her ankles, but when she walked towards the front door they did not follow. With a sense of trouble, Patsy let herself into the dark house.

It was cold. That was the first thing she noticed, and there was no murmur from the central heating pump. The light came on, though, when she pressed the switch, although she had half expected it not to. Something had wrecked the decorations. Holly lay on the floor, and the tree was overturned, earth from the pot she had planted it in strewn across the carpet. Tinsel shimmered from the floor, and the Rayburn door hung open, showing that the fire was out.

'Oh no.' Patsy sank into the armchair in the corner, the warm happiness of a shared Christmas evaporating at once. 'No...why? Your mother...I hear she didn't like Christmas, but...but I live here now. Oh Emrys...how...how could you? It...it isn't fair.'

The cold, and the ruin of her decorations, and the thought of re-lighting the stove, while outside all the evening chores still waited, were all too much. Patsy began to cry. It was no use, she would have to give in...she should never have come here, it was hard enough making a dream become real life without an extra problem like Emrys.

Outside Goliath roared again, and the mare whinnied. Patsy took a deep breath and pulled herself to her feet. It had to be done, and there was no-one else. At the very least the horses must be fed, hayed, watered, and skipped out.

It was cold in the yard, cold and raw, with a nasty little wind meeting her at the corners. With little heart for it Patsy plodded through the chores, pausing for a minute at the end in Goliath's stable, an arm over his comfortable, warm neck while he contentedly munched hay. At least Emrys didn't upset the horses, and even the cats half-accepted him. Giving the old skewbald horse a final stroke Patsy turned back to the house.

Going into the back room she stopped dead in astonishment. The Christmas tree was upright again, although rather lop-sided, and most of the earth was back in the pot. Some of the holly was back in place, and odd strands of tinsel hung in rather odd places. Emrys had tried to make amends. The sheer unexpectedness of it made Patsy want to laugh, but she knew that this was not the right reaction.

'Thank you,' she said, instead. 'Thank you Emrys.'

She re-lit the stove, which burned up immediately, finished replacing the decorations, and answered the telephone to Katy, who was ringing to make sure that her mother had survived Christmas without her. Then she made herself a sandwich with the slices of turkey which Rhiannon had insisted she took home with her and settled down by the stove, with two of the reassured cats on her knee. There was no presence in the room now, and Patsy knew that Emrys, as seemed to be the way after any extra surge of energy, was no longer there.

It was sleeting the next morning, a cold, thin wetness which left small piles of soft ice in corners, harried there by the bitter wind. The hills were hidden by the low cloud, and the mare and foal stood tucked under the hedge while Goliath, stabled, yelled for food and to be let out. When Patsy did turn him out, however, he did not like it, hurrying to shelter and then standing beside the other two ponies with a look of utter disgust about him. The cats had refused to come outside at all, and sheltering birds hopped around Patsy's feet, waiting for pickings, as she mucked out and swept up. Jackdaws were the boldest, apart from the robins, strutting close by, crooning to one another, keeping in their couples as they always did, while the robins perched on the barrow and doors, pausing in their watch for food to swoop down and attack one another in furious defence of territories.

Patsy found the work hard going. Her legs felt leaden this morning, and by the time she went indoors for a coffee she knew that she had the beginnings of a sore throat. She would stay indoors as much as possible, she decided, as going down with anything worse than a cold would mean begging for help, and she was determined not to do that if at all possible.

By evening the clouds had lifted, and a hard frost was setting in. In the last of the light the hills glistened white where the sleet, higher up, had become snow, and the yard had slippery patches of ice in unexpected places. Shivering, and feeling sore all over, Patsy brought all the horses in, fed them, and plodded back into the house, to the warmth of the stove and the cats piled on her knee. A can of soup was enough for supper, and then she crawled into bed with two hot water bottles and the same pile of cats, who were only too pleased to share any warmth going.

After a miserable night, alternately hot and cold, Patsy knew that she had flu. The sensible thing to do would be telephone Rhiannon, and ask for help, but when she looked outside she saw that the clouds had returned, and it was snowing properly. John and Rhiannon would have their hands full with the milking and bringing their own stock into shelter, apart from the probability that the roads would be treacherous even for the short distance from the farm. Pulling on extra sweaters and her thickest jacket and woolly hat, Patsy ventured unsteadily out into the weather.

If she had felt well it would have been an experience to remember. The snow blew down the yard and across the fields in waves, lying soft and deepening under foot, and the stables and barns were full of sheltering birds. There were rabbits in the warmth of the hay, burrows less used these days after myxomatosis, and a strong smell of fox and paw-prints in blown snow showed that the 'thief of the world' had not been slow to see his chance. The horses seemed happy to stay in, and Patsy left mucking out, merely giving them plenty of hay and fresh water. Her legs felt so weak that as she faced the walk back to the house in the teeth of the wind she was doubtful of making it.

'Rubbish,' she told herself, as briskly as she could. 'It's only about fifty yards.'

She made it, but once indoors the thought of cleaning the Rayburn and going outside again for coal was just too much. Taking the small electric fire with her, Patsy returned to bed.

She did not know much about that day, until Goliath's usual demanding yell dragged her out of bed on legs that felt about to give way, and down the stairs. At the bottom she knew that it was no use: she would have to telephone Rhiannon. She picked up the 'phone, and listened in dismay to the silence. No ringing tone...the line must be down...somehow she must feed and water her charges on her own.

Outside the snow was deep and starting to freeze in the still bitterly blowing wind. It was almost dark, only the snow light showing Patsy the way across the yard, as she had forgotten to bring a torch. Pressing the switch for the yard lights brought no response, and with a mounting feeling of dull dread Patsy realised that behind her the house lights were off. It was not only the telephone lines that were down, in the last few minutes the power, mostly supplied by overhead cables, was also out.

Feeling that every step was a mile, with the sheaves of hay weighing a ton, Patsy succeeded in getting the horses fed. Water was impossible...the yard tap was frozen, and she knew that there was no way she could carry filled buckets from the house, even if the indoor tap was still working. None of the buckets were quite empty, they must just manage until the morning. Surely by then she would feel a little better.

The night was full of nightmares, the cold crept in, and between bouts of sweating Patsy shivered uncontrollably, coughing and breathless. The cats, disgusted by the noise, deserted her, and Patsy swallowed paracetamol and tried to believe that she would feel better in the morning, if it ever came.

It did, of course, light creeping through the curtains, bright, unearthly snow light, and yells from the horses. The old cat returned, landing on Patsy's stomach to announce that it was breakfast time, and too cold for hunting. The telephone was still dead, and Patsy staggered down the stairs, knowing that she could not let the horses stand starving in their stables.

She hardly knew anything about that day, the almost impossible task of getting water to the horses from the thankfully still running indoor tap, the struggle in the still blowing wind to get hay to the horses, and the bitter cold in the unheated house. Thinking that she would drive for help she tried to start the car, but it was dead, the cold too much for the battery. By dusk Patsy knew that she could not go on much longer. The horses were waiting, once again, for hay, and indoors the cats, puzzled and upset by the cold and their usually attentive mistress's failure to feed them at their usual time, huddled in a resentful group on the cold stove.

Very slowly, Patsy made her way down the yard in the wind and the flying specks of icy snow, to the hay barn. Inside, she was sheltered, and Patsy sank down onto a bale of hay, soft and faintly warm. She would rest for a few minutes before the day's final effort. It was warmer than the house, and gratefully she closed her eyes and let her aching muscles sink into the sweet softness. As soon as her eyes were closed dreams took over, dreams or hallucinations, she was not sure which, or worried about it. There was Katy somewhere, out of reach as Patsy called her, David, coming towards her over a green field, but suddenly the ground opened and he vanished, falling with a despairing cry. And then the nightmares faded, there was a quietness, and a light, edging in, and Patsy could see Emrys, standing with his back to the light. Suddenly she knew what he had to do.

'Turn round,' she struggled to tell him. 'Turn...look at the light...look away from here...'

Outside, in the real world, the wind picked up, sending snow thudding down from the barn roof, and spraying Patsy with cold particles, and Goliath yelled, anxious about the failure of his tea to arrive. Patsy felt cold and pain flooding back, and opened her eyes. The yard was dark, but she could still see a figure, outlined against the gleaming snow light...a stocky figure with hand held out towards her.

'Come with me,' she heard again. 'This time, you can come...'

'Y...yes...perhaps...' Patsy could feel the sweet pull of peace and light, and behind Emrys again the light was growing. Patsy was starting to hold out her own hand to reach the offered one when the light grew brighter, dazzling, and became the headlights of a vehicle bumping and sliding carefully across the icy cattle grid into the yard. For a moment she could still see Emrys, and she saw him start to turn, and then he was gone. Reality was back, as two people got out of the Land Rover and began to slide hastily towards her.

'Mum...'it was Katy's voice, scared and anxious. 'Mum...are you all right? Gareth, something's wrong...'

'Get her indoors,' Gareth, astonishingly it was Gareth, was bending over her. 'I can carry her, you go and organise some heat, and use your mobile for an ambulance.'

'I don't want...'Patsy tried to say, but a bout of painful coughing took over, and she had to give in to the indignity of being carried across the yard and into the house, where Katy was stuffing newspaper and kindling into the open Rayburn. Sat on a chair, wrapped in blankets, Patsy felt reality swimming away again, back into dreams and memories of light and Emrys, of David and of Richard, her husband. She had no idea how long it was before she opened her eyes properly to cool hospital lighting, a white bed in a curtained corner of a ward, and an efficient nurse bending over her.

Later, sitting up in bed and starting to recover, Katy explained.

'Gareth's course was in London,' she said. 'He 'phoned me and told me Bethan had broken it off, and asked to meet. We've been seeing each other ever since. I...I wanted to tell you...then I hoped you'd come for Christmas and see for yourself, but it didn't happen. We agreed to come down on Boxing Day, and see you and Gareth's family, but the snow was too bad. We made it today, and when we got to the farm Rhiannon was about to set off to see if you were all right, since the 'phones were down. We came instead.'

'Just in time,' admitted Patsy. 'I'm really glad about you and Gareth. Er...is Andrew really forgotten?'

'Definitely,' Katy looked down. 'I was a fool about Andrew, wasn't I? Knowing Gareth made me realise that. He'll be coming back to work in Carmarthen after his course, and...and I'm going to get a job round here as well. We...we really want to be together now, and I'm fed up with living in the south-east when there's all this space and air down here. We've been staying at Bryn Uchaf, by the way; old Emrys doesn't seem to care.'

'I think he's learned his lesson,' Patsy told her. 'Don't interfere.'

Back home a week later Patsy went rather unsteadily out into the yard. Everything was peaceful, the horses nibbling the brownish winter grass, from which the snow had cleared. It was a bright day, the hills sparkling clear against the pale sky, and as Patsy leaned on the gate she was aware that she was not alone.

'Go on,' she said softly. 'I did show you the way, didn't I? One day, I'll follow, but not yet. Goodbye Emrys.'

There was no reply, but Patsy thought that she felt a light touch on her shoulder, no more than a breath of wind. Then it was gone. The light in the field seemed to sparkle for a moment, a stir in the atmosphere, and the horses raised their heads and pricked their ears. A cool wind swept over Patsy, and then the air and the light settled. She was really alone: she would not meet Emrys again in this world. Rather sadly she turned, hearing Katy call from the kitchen. It was time to pick up the threads again, and carry on, for however long she had.

EPILOGUE...FOUR YEARS LATER

It was a hot day in July. The Royal Welsh Show was in full swing, and crammed. It was Wednesday, cob day, when the whole of Wales seemed to be packed into the great temporary village that was the show at Builth Wells. Standing close to the ropes, a place she had claimed from the moment the class for stallions in hand began, Patsy was chewing her nails. In the ring stood two rows of stamping, sidling, head-tossing Welsh cob stallions, prideful arrogance and fire blazing from even the least impressive of them, and trotting up past the judges for their final decision was Hedfa Aur, fully mature, a gleaming, flashing chestnut, his pale mane flying like flames along his arched, muscular crest, his long, crinkly tail held high, stepping out in his huge, powerful, elevated trot in time with the flashing white trainers on the feet of Gareth, running him out. At the entrance to the collecting ring Katy too was watching intently, and as the judge raised his hat and held it out towards Hedfa Aur five minutes later Patsy saw the blazing delight in her daughter's face, equal only to her own. Best stallion at the Royal Welsh, a proud title indeed. And when, later in the day, Hedfa Aur stood out supreme champion of all the cobs, youngstock, mares, and stallions, to win the most coveted award in Wales, the Prince of Wales cup, Patsy could only wonder amid her pride and delight, if Emrys knew.

Someday, when they did meet again, if such things were possible, she would tell him...if things so earthly still mattered then, and surely, to those who had loved and worked for them, they would.

Printed in Great Britain
by Amazon